Elke's Magic

INGER MARGARET FOSTER

"Love recognizes no barriers. It jumps hurdles, leaps fences, penetrates walls to arrive at its destination full of hope."

~Maya Angelou

Printed by King Printing Co., Inc., Lowell, Massachusetts

Cover and interior book layout design by Karen Busch Holman of Hwin and Little Bear Press Edited by JMG
ISBN: 978-17325969-5-5

Photos by inger

"Hwin and Little Bear" photos courtesy of

Karen Busch Holman

PROLOGUE

Once mutual vows and simple rings had been shared, there was time only for a quick yet tender embrace. Apprehension mixed with relief as the hurried and clandestine ceremony concluded. Afterwards they all went about their day as if nothing out of the ordinary had even occurred.

They had to. No one outside of the immediate family could know what had transpired that morning. The consequences alone of what they had all been part of had created complications too unbelievable, too illegal, to explain.

CHAPTER 1

THE DEER

Elke placed a small brown ceramic bowl just outside the oak door, leaving it slightly ajar while she waited behind it, listening. Moments later she heard the tentative tap-tap tapping of hooves as the animal she was waiting for slowly climbed the steps up onto the front porch. Limping and favoring her front left leg, the creature made its way to the bowl and began rapidly licking the cooled liquid. Ever so silently, the woman moved closer. The doe then lowered herself to the wooden floor, head nodding to her chest.

Elke waited until the deep liquid brown eyes had closed completely and the animal had fallen into a gentle slumber. Kneeling directly in front of her, she took the injured leg into her hands. Feeling along the femur, she located the injury, as a soft violet light emanated from its source. Alternately massaging and firmly holding the leg, she looked up into the clear blue sky, sending whispered healing words into the universe.

The doe stayed there, inert, for a few more minutes. And then, as if awakened from a loud noise, her eyes opened suddenly. She looked deeply into the azure blue eyes of the woman in front of her, unblinkingly holding the gaze until the woman nodded. Bowing her head ever so slightly, the deer rose up from the white-washed deck and trotted off slowly. Then, after stopping and turning back to look at the woman one more time, she kicked up her back hooves, raised her fluffy white tail and bounded off into the forest.

Closing the door, Elke went back into the kitchen, sitting down heavily on the padded chair at her little cherry wood table to finish her lukewarm cup of tea. A little black cat wove around her ankles, mewing softly to get her attention. Absentmindedly petting his soft and furry head, she gave him a final scratch behind the ear. Leaning against the table, she pushed herself up to stand, and went to the cupboard for his food.

"There you go, Midnight. Enjoy your supper."

Tonight's dinner, simmering on the cast iron stove, was almost ready. The loaf of bread had risen, and she placed it into the oven. Moving slowly and gingerly, she set the table for two. Healings were painful for her, afterward, but the pain left eventually. It just took a little longer sometimes. She folded two red plaid fringed napkins and placed them next to the forks. Victor would be home soon, back from soccer practice. As always, he would be ravenous.

Tending to the supper, she stirred the stew until it was cooked through, removing it from the burner. At that exact moment, the cottage door opened behind her, and she turned to great the lanky young man as he carefully wiped the mud from his shoes on the black rubber door mat. His blond head nearly touched the top of the door frame and he had to duck a bit as he entered the little cottage. He placed his school books and a small packet of mail on the kitchen counter. Towering over his petite mother, he leaned down, giving her a quick hug.

They ate companionably. Victor talked a bit about school and practice. They had a big game tomorrow. "I hope you can come, Mom. It starts at four, if you are finished at work."

"Of course! I wouldn't miss it for the world! I can escape a bit early."

Elke regaled her son with stories from her own day's activities, filling him in on the antics of a few ornery patients made even more miserable by a cranky sleep-deprived intern. She mentioned running into one of his friend's mothers who was visiting a patient. And then she stopped herself right before she blurted out what just happened on the porch. Yes, she would skip that part. She couldn't tell him about the deer. Undoubtedly, he would roll his eyes.

Knowing that Victor was a bit dubious about what she was actually doing, she kept the facts about the healings to herself. All he knew was that she did something or other to help the woodland creatures or any other animal that mysteriously appeared at their doorstep. The list went on and on. There was the hawk that arrived one afternoon, with an injured wing. He flew off later, into the sunset, but still stopped by daily for a greeting. He would actually allow Elke to pet him. And then there was that rabbit that appeared just before delivering her litter, who of course she had assisted with the difficult birth. They all lived safely under the porch, multiplying constantly. And then there were their own pets, all just showing up either on their own, or dropped off in the middle of the night by perfect strangers.

Often Victor would catch her midstream, in the midst of helping the animals. Uncomfortable, he would quickly look the other way. Understanding his reactions, though, even though it bothered her a bit, she got it. Yes, it was simply too strange, too far fetched. One day he confided in her that it would be totally mortifying if his friends knew. "Mom, he had said, "I love you. But they won't understand. Here we are, just the two of us, tucked away deep in the forest in a little cottage. Surrounded by animals. Exactly like a fairytale."

He never brought anyone home, always making excuses.

Elke knew that he would someday understand what she did. Eventually. She had been hesitant herself in the beginning. It was indeed quite unfathomable. This gift, even though she did not think of it as such, was just a part of her. It was who she was and what she was. Still, it was something that had taken her ages to accept. And so she knew it would take time for Victor as well.

Finishing up the last bite of his stew and dipping the end of the bread in to soak up the delicious sauce, he stood up and turned to his mother. "Thanks Mom. Great meal." He stacked and then cleared the plates. Grabbing his books, he climbed the stairs, but turned back towards her, saying apologetically over his shoulder, "Sorry for the rush. Lots of homework tonight."

"Honey, no need to feel badly. Go. We'll talk in the morning."

Finishing the dishes quickly, Elke grabbed her shawl before she headed out. Time to take care of the rest of the household before it got too late. She opened the back door and called out into the slowly darkening night.

"Madison, Scout, it's time for bed!"

The two horses were on the far side of the paddock and they both looked up nonchalantly at the sound of her voice. Impishly ignoring her, they lowered their heads again to get in a few more last minute nibbles from the grass sprouting up along the perimeter of the paddock. She called once more and waited patiently, gathering her shawl more tightly around her, guarding against the chill in the air. The sun was just setting over the open field. Shadows were forming around the thickly wooded forest, an ink wash darkly muting the lines, giving one the feeling of being surrounded and protected by castle walls.

"Last call, girls."

The liver chestnut mare came first, trotting along the side of the paddock toward the barn. Right behind her was a miniature horse, trying ever so hard to keep pace. Elke greeted them both with a hug and a kiss each, and gently led them into their stalls. Adding water to the troughs, she mixed together their special meal, a combination of herbs and grains.

"Goodnight, my girls." Elke gave each horse one last hug as she covered them with their matching red blankets, one quite a bit smaller than the other. She closed the barn door with a click and headed back into the cottage just as the sun sank deeply behind the forest.

CHAPTER 2

THE COTTAGE

It was always hard to sleep past the rooster and his morning wake-up call. Rising with a stretch, Elke tucked her feet into the slippers placed under her bed and grabbed her fuzzy green bathrobe, tying it tightly around her waist to keep warm. She could see her breath in the air as she quietly made her way down the creaky wooden stairs to the kitchen. Victor would sleep for another hour at least.

Fall was most certainly here. She added kindling and wood to the stove, and lit it with a long wooden match. She then filled the coffee pot, measured out the exact amount and put the pot on to perk. She was running low on coffee. She added it in chalk to the list on the little black board hanging near the back door.

Warming her hands with the heat coming from the crackling flames, she waited patiently for the coffee to finish perking. Then, later, as she sipped her beverage, she listed in her mind the things she needed to take care of that day. Reluctantly, she headed upstairs to take her morning shower, wishing she could have lingered a bit longer near the stove's warmth. Dressing quickly into her uniform in the still chilly home, she pushed herself forward.

Grabbing the basket at the back door, she stepped into her black rubber boots and put on her red plaid woolen coat. Impatiently, Midnight squeezed his way through the door as soon as it was ajar. She paused, as she always did, once the door was completely open. This time, and every single time she looked out, she was completely amazed at how very beautiful it was. It was magical. Always.

The early morning sunlight was just beginning to penetrate the fog as it gradually lifted through the trees. Sparkling dew covered the grass. And even though she wished her days didn't have to begin so very early, she loved the serenity of the start of each and every morning.

Entering the coop, Elke stopped by each hen, removing eggs from underneath their soft and warm perches, greeting them by name. There were four little brown hens. Sally, Sandy, Susie and Sabrina. Of course, there was Sam, the ever protective and very vocal rooster, warily watching her every move. She knew she was being overly alliterative with her names for the brood, but it was fun saying them, making her laugh to herself as her tongue tied when she said them all very quickly.

Next it was off to the barn. Midnight scooted into the cozy building, popping in to greet Madison and Scout. They both gave him soft nuzzles as he curled around their hooves, purring. Then, it was time for the cat to explore the hay pile, looking for any mice that might still be scurrying about, before the sun rose higher in the sky.

After feeding the horses, Elke led the pair back out into the paddock. The sun had just peeked up over the trees, and its warmth was welcomed. She turned and headed back inside to start breakfast.

While two of the fresh brown eggs poached, she sliced thick pieces of yesterday's freshly baked bread, and buttered them generously. Grabbing another cup of coffee, she set the food on the table. Victor would be downstairs soon.

CHAPTER 3

HUDSON

"Hello?" The voice was hesitant, almost a whisper.

It was early Saturday morning, and Elke had been deep in thought, pulling the last of the carrots out of the garden behind the cottage. A deja vu, yet not quite a deja vu. For she had done this before, so many times, in a place so far away and a time so long ago.

A bit startled, as she was rarely taken off guard, she turned and looked back from her kneeling position. There were two young girls, directly behind her. One looked to be about eleven or twelve. The other maybe thirteen, most likely fourteen. One taller than the other. The smaller one was blond, the taller one a redhead. The older girl was holding a cat. She looked deeply concerned.

"Hi, I'm Meg. This is my sister, Sarah and this is Hudson. He is having trouble breathing. Can you help us?"

Elke stood up, slowly, as the joints in her knees were tight, still aching from the healing a few days before. Without looking at the girls, she directed all of her focus on the black and white Tuxedo cat. Yes, there was something definitely wrong.

"Follow me," she directed them, taking the cat into her arms. She headed back to the cottage, as quickly as she could. The girls followed right behind her.

The cat, limp in Elke's arms, was barely breathing and gasping with each and every breath. She laid him on her kitchen counter and began massaging his chest. Without stopping, she gave the girls directions. "Meg, could you open that jar right there. No, not that one, the next one. Yes, that's it. Thank you. Okay. Now Sarah, see that pot on the stove? The water in it is still hot. Be careful. Use a pot holder. Carefully pour some of that water into one of the ceramic bowls drying right there in the drain board. Slowly. Now, Meg, please add a pinch of the herbs from the jar into the water."

Meg added the herbs to the hot water and its gentle scent filled the air.

"It's sage, oregano and thyme. And bay leaf. It will help open Hudson's airways. Here, bring that closer so he can breathe it in."

She really didn't need the girls to make the brew. She just needed to distract them to keep them busy and unaware of what she was actually doing. Although the herbs did help, it wasn't what was most needed.

The little cat started to breathe a bit more freely. He looked up into Elke's eyes, just for a moment before he closed them again, tightly. Elke continued to work her magic, gently urging and moving what she knew was an obstruction. Blocking the view so that the girls could not see the violet light glowing near his chest cavity, Elke massaged the area. Then she quickly hooked the cat over her shoulder, patting his back like one would do after feeding a newborn baby. First came a cough, and then choking. Something then dropped onto the floor. It was a button. "There, there, my little friend. You will be just fine." Elke cradled the cat, stoking his back. Meg and Sarah smiled with joy.

"Here he is, girls. As good as new. Well almost! Best to keep him away from the sewing box in the future! Now. How did you find me?" Elke handed the cat to the older girl, and sat down, exhausted, at the little table.

"We were looking for our cat, Mrs....Wait. We don't know your name."

"Oh, I am so sorry. How rude of me. My name is Elke Becker."

"Mrs. Becker. Wait. Are you Vic's mom?" Elke thought she noticed that Meg's fair and freckled skin looked a little redder. Like she was blushing.

"Why yes I am!"

On cue, Victor appeared on the staircase, sleepy eyed and rumpled. Seeing the backs of two young girls, he did an immediate about-face and headed back up, before they noticed. Elke noticed him though, and while she listened attentively to Meg, she laughed a bit to herself.

"Anyway, we live near the lake in town." Meg, oblivious to the fleeting presence of Victor, stammered it all out, almost breathlessly. "We were in the woods across the street from our house, looking for Hudson. He never ate his breakfast this morning. He had disappeared and wasn't coming home when we called him. He never does that. Well, we caught sight of him heading this way. We kept walking and walking. And then we weren't sure where we were. We were sort of lost. Well, I guess we were really lost. Then, we saw a patch of light and that was where we found him, just near the clearing. We were just going to try to find our way back when we saw you and your house. We didn't know that Vic, I mean, you, I mean you both, lived up here."

Elke knew that Hudson must have been trying to find her. For healing. And also that her son, Victor, must have had some kind of effect on this girl, sometime in the past. She just nodded her head. But she didn't say a word. About either subject.

"How can we ever thank you, Mrs. Becker?" Sarah asked the woman.

"Well, now, let me think. Hmm. Do you girls like horses?" Elke looked right at the two of them, and couldn't help smiling herself as she saw the happy grins spreading across their faces. "Come." Elke beckoned. "You need to meet my friends."

Elke led them both out to the barn, and introduced them to her equine friends. "Meg, Sarah, this is Scout," She is a miniature horse. And this is Madison." Elke pulled the fifteen and a half hand horse gently from her stall. "Madison would love to have someone ride her. Victor is too busy with soccer, and I am just too exhausted after my long days at work to ride much anymore."

"But Mrs. Becker, we don't know how to ride. We have never even been on a horse." Sarah said, as she turned away from the little horse's side and looked up into Elke's eyes.

"No worries! I will teach you! Please come. Anytime. I only work weekdays until around four o'clock. Other than that I am always here. And I love surprise visits!"

The girls tentatively petted the horses soft muzzles, loving their gentle natures. Elke handed each girl a few baby carrots, and the horses gobbled up the treats. Both girls giggled after getting ticklish nuzzles of thanks in return.

Reluctantly they turned to Elke to say their goodbyes, Meg scooping up Hudson, who had followed them into the barn. Elke told them to wait a moment, and went back into the house to draw a simple map that showed the easy route back through the woods. She then sent the girls and their cat on their way, knowing for certain that they would return. She turned and headed back to the house to start making a late breakfast for her son, thinking that things were about to become rather interesting.

CHAPTER 4

ELKE

Elke brushed her white-blond hair and braided it into one long tail that trailed down her spine. Smiling at her reflection, she thought about what was about to transpire. Heading down to the kitchen, she quickly washed up the breakfast dishes, and then went out to the barn.

"Madison, Scout, you have visitors coming! They will be here soon!"

It was Sunday morning, and it was a beautiful autumn day. Meg and Sarah were on their way. She could feel it in the air.

Pulling out the curry comb and brushes, she started grooming her little horse first, whispering endearing words into her velvety soft ear. Knowing that the girls had just come into the clearing, she stopped for a moment, and then went back to work so that it would look as though it were indeed going to be a surprise visit.

"Hello, Mrs. Becker!" Meg had called, stopping just outside the barn.

Elke feigned a startled jump and looked back at the two figures framed by the barn door, silhouetted in the glow of the sunshine behind them.

"Oh, good, you made it! And you found your way a bit more easily this time?"

They came over for quick hugs. "Yes! Thanks for the map, Mrs. Becker." Meg said, smiling. "It really is direct and simple once you know where you are going."

"For sure! Victor often hikes through the woods that way when he goes to the lake and to town. He was the one who discovered the route, ages ago. And your parents? Are they all right with you coming here?"

The two girls looked at each other, surreptitiously, and then both smiled and nodded, almost too simultaneously.

"Good. All right then." A bit worried, as it was obvious that they were not quite telling the truth, she decided to go ahead with the plans anyway, hoping for the best. She was a mother, too. She would make it all work out, and hopefully smooth over any problems should they occur.

"Okay. Let's start with the basics," Elke led them to Scout's side. "This is how you groom." Elke showed the girls how to carefully brush, curry and comb the horse before she handed Meg the brush. Holding onto the top of Meg's hand, she indicated the proper pressure needed to get through Scout's rather tangly mane. Doing the same with Sarah, she guided her to the less heavy coat along the horse's flanks.

"It is really important to develop a relationship with a horse, before one actually gets in the saddle. Grooming the horse is, I think, a lovely way to start that friendship. They need to trust you. We will get Scout all neat and tidy, and then move on to Madison. Madison is really protective of her little friend, which is why I always groom her first."

Watching how the girls approached their task was a joy for Elke. But she noticed that they seemed to drag it out a bit too long. Inherently knowing that they were intimidated by the much larger Madison looming above them, she realized that she would have to approach things differently.

"Being a bit afraid of a large animal is not a bad thing. One actually should be wary." Seeing the look of relief on both of their faces, she went on. "Foolishness leads to danger, and I would prefer you were more hesitant than overly confident. If you take the approach too lightly, there is a greater chance of injury occurring. Let me show you how to handle this rather large creature." Elke moved closer to Madison, and whispered into her ear. Turning back to the girls, she continued. "Here, Meg, just hold your hand with the brush right here, and do exactly what you were doing with Scout. Oh, and talk to her."

Meg's nervousness appeared to fade, and, with her usually chatty way, she talked and talked to Madison as though she were having a conversation with a close friend. Initial apprehension turned into mutual trust. Sarah joined in, following Meg's lead.

Soon they were all finished, and Elke demonstrated how to place the saddle and bridal on Madison. "Okay, this is a bit of a trick, but horses often puff out their stomachs after the initial fastening of the saddle. So, we wait a bit, and then give it another tightening. One doesn't want to fall off, and that can certainly happen with a loose saddle!"

Elke examined their handiwork. "Perfect. Now that the hard work is complete, it's time for some fun. But before we do that, come over here and grab a helmet from the rack. There are several there, and you should be able to find one that fits. Never ride without one! Also, today is fine as you have on sneakers and we are just beginning, but in time you will need proper equestrian boots and breeches." Smiling at them both, she added, "And I certainly hope you will want to keep on riding!"

Holding the horse's bridal, Elke led the mount out into the paddock. Leading her over to a wooden step, she motioned for the girls to come. Following right behind the girls was Scout, nosily watching their every move.

"Meg, let's start with you first. Step up here, and then swing this leg over. Place your toes right here, and I will adjust the stirrups. Each rider is different, and so the stirrups need to be the proper length. Is this comfortable?"

When Meg nodded, Elke went on. "Take the reins, just like this." Showing her how to hold the reins in her hands, firmly yet lightly, she continued with her instruction. "Reins are sort of like the horse's steering wheel. Guide Madison with your hands, and also by pressing your legs into her sides."

Before Meg ventured out into the paddock, Elke explained the saddle. "This is called an English saddle. I first learned to ride on a saddle similar to this, when I was Sarah's age. English style riding is what you will be learning."

Tracing her hand over the front of the saddle, Elke pointed out how form fitting it was, and how it actually hugged the contours of Madison's back. "It is quite different from a Western saddle. I am sure you have seen that type, in movies and such. A Western saddle is heavier and bigger, with a pommel in the front that one can hold onto. Many think that it is much easier to ride Western. Especially on trails or rough terrain. However, since the English saddle is lighter and smaller, the rider is able to have better contact with the horse's back. All that being said, the saddle's good qualities do create more of a challenging ride. That is why it is important to have someone teach you properly."

Elke went on, explaining to both girls. "We will start Madison off with a walk, while you acclimate yourself to your seat, which is a term for how you are placed in the saddle. Then, we will put Madison into a trot and you will move with a technique called posting. It will make your ride smoother, otherwise you will be bumping all about. I will tell you when to rise. Wait for when I say 'post' and just raise up slightly. In time your body will fall into a rhythm with Madison, and you will move up and down accordingly, in time with the gait of the horse. It really is fun!"

At first, Meg's laps around the paddock were understandably awkward. Making corrections calmly yet firmly, Elke helped Meg understand how her own moves affected the horse, and vice versa. Eventually rider and mount would become one. In time.

"That was great, Meg. I think you are a natural!" Elke helped her dismount. Then it was Sarah's turn.

The moment Sarah lifted her left leg over the horse's back, Elke knew something was not quite right. She kept an eye on the girl as she went through the motions, and led her through a similar lesson. However, she kept things simpler. One, because Sarah was younger. And two, Elke had concerns for the younger girl. Worried, she stopped the lesson a bit earlier than she had anticipated.

"Okay, girls! That was wonderful! You both did really well. I can't believe it was your first time on horseback. Let's bring Madison back into her stall."

The trio brought Madison inside again, and Elke showed them how to remove the saddle and bridle. She then demonstrated how to rub down the horses sweaty flanks. They brushed her again. Afterwards, Elke showed them the correct way to muck out the stalls.

As she scooped the manure into a wheelbarrow, she turned back to look at the girls. "You know, some people think that horses and barns smell badly. I guess maybe they do, but you get used to it after a while and then you don't really even notice it. I actually kind of like the smell, as strange as that might sound! Maybe it is because I love the animals so much. It all goes with the territory."

"It's not too terrible! The smell, I mean." Meg said, and then added, "That was so much fun! When can we come back, Mrs. Becker? Ooh, I am sorry that sounded so rude. May we please come back again?"

"Not rude at all and of course! Next week. Sunday is perfect for me, but see how your week goes to see which day is best for you. Okay. Enough work. Let's go in for a much needed drink." Elke brought the girls to the mudroom and showed them where to wash their hands. "You will be a bit messy and muddy after riding, and you may have some aches and pains in your legs, but that is all normal. You will get used to it!"

Once in the kitchen, Elke handed them each a tall glass of apple cider. "That's from my first batch this year from the apple trees near the stable." Pointing to the basket of slightly bruised apples near the back door, she added, "We can go out and bring apple treats to the horses before you head home."

They finished their cider, and Elke gathered the glasses and placed them in the old farm sink, running the faucet to give them a quick rinse. Pausing at the counter, Elke hesitated before she again spoke. She knew, though, that she had to broach the next subject carefully. "Sarah, did you have a recent injury?"

Sarah looked first at Meg, and then at Elke.

"Yes, Mrs. Becker. Well, not too recently." Sarah looked down for a moment and then added, "Actually I was hit by a car, about two years ago. Around Christmas time. I broke my leg." Then she got up quickly from the table, as if to abruptly change the subject. "The cider was delicious, Mrs. Becker. Thank you so much for everything."

"Actually I should be thanking you! You helped me so much with the horses today." Elke knew now was not the time to prod for more information. The right time would occur. Soon. She hoped.

Heading back out the door, Meg and Sarah each grabbed an apple. Stopping by the barn, they approached the two horses before leaving. Both horses eagerly accepted the gifts, nuzzling their new friends. Then the girls went on their way, thanking Elke again.

Elke, as she watched them make their way to the path, tenderly stroked the side of the mare's neck, whispering, "My darling Madison, we must help that girl."

CHAPTER 5

LESSONS

Meg and Sarah made it to Elke's every Sunday after that. They told her that was the day they could get away the easiest, the day when they had less responsibilities and activities. With the consistency of the lessons, coupled with their kind and patient teacher, they were making progress in no time. Becoming more and more proficient in their riding skills, Elke made sure that her attentive students were challenged, and she pushed them to excel.

After the lessons, the three would all go into Elke's cozy kitchen and have cider or tea and freshly baked cookies. Enjoying their visits immensely, she began to learn more and more about the girls, as they started filling her in on the basic details of their life at home and at school. They took ballet twice a week, and they also were in the band at the middle school. Meg, in eighth grade, played the clarinet, Sarah, in sixth, played the flute. By listening more than speaking, Elke shared only glimpses into her own very private life.

Elke's openness paved the way for the girls to share more easily. However, the two would often catch themselves, mid-sentence, changing direction in topic. Actions spoke the loudest. Unvoiced words whispered the truth. Through their body language, and more importantly through what was left unspoken, it was apparent to Elke that their life at home was often strained. From Elke's perspective, Meg appeared to be the mother figure. The elder sister was completely protective of the younger one, even though only two years separated them. However strange it had appeared to her, Elke actually wondered if it were indeed perfectly normal, this protective older sibling thing. Perhaps it was akin to how Madison looked out for Scout.

Or maybe it was just a sisterly role, happening within a typical family. But how was she to know? As atypical as her own family had been, she had been an only child. Well, at least she had been an only child for years. Until she was taken in by the Becker family. In that family, though, she was more of a friend than a sister to the other children. Technically that did not count.

This sisterly dynamic intrigued her, though. Coupled with her own only-child-status was the fact that she had given birth to only one child herself. So she wasn't exactly privy to the vagaries of having or being an actual sibling. Seeing the Pedersens' relationship made her wonder if she should have perhaps had more children. She regretted, a bit, that she had never given Victor a brother of sister. But that had not been in the cards for her. Never had it even been an option.

As of late, Elke noticed Victor was beginning to hang around a bit more on Sundays. Leaning against the fence, he would often watch the lessons. Trying to look nonchalant, but actually failing miserably, he gave the appearance of one who was riveted. Or smitten. There was something more going on than just curiosity. Something was in the air. Perhaps.

One Sunday, Victor had saddled up Madison, and began a ride around the ring, just before the appointed time for the girls to arrive. Coming out of the barn, Elke watched him show off from afar, even though he would never have acknowledged it as showing off. He would justify it as simply having had an urge to ride.

Meg and Sarah had stopped in their tracks, and were standing by the paddock. So engrossed in the display before them, they didn't even notice that Elke had come over to join them, and was currently standing right behind them. Meg literally jumped when she heard Elke's voice. "He is pretty good, no?" Apparently a bit dumbstruck, Meg had a hard time speaking coherently and muttered something unintelligible.

Over the next few weeks, Elke sat back a bit, enjoying the developing relationship. Leaving the three alone, she let things unfold naturally. All of them were really getting along. Sometimes Victor helped the sisters with the grooming and saddling, and they would banter back and forth, gently teasing each other. Mostly Meg and Victor. But they were both kind enough to include Sarah.

It was nice, having them around. It felt like family.

At one point, Victor had confided in his mother that he felt badly for not having recognized Meg at all. Even as he got to know her better, nothing had stood out as ever having known her in the past. Yet she had seemed to know all about him. Assuring Victor that this was not at all an issue, she reminded him that they had been two years apart while attending middle school. Most eighth graders rarely noticed sixth graders. However it would not have been unusual in the reverse. Things would undoubtedly be different in the near future, Elke knew. Victor was currently a sophomore at Beauville High. Meg would begin her freshman year next September. Elke secretly hoped that they would connect again. She really liked this girl and she assumed, or maybe she knew, that her son did as well.

CHAPTER 6

MEG

One Sunday, over cups of tea and shortbread cookies, Meg approached Elke with something that had been puzzling her. As always, when she was a bit hesitant or nervous, she spewed it all out in a torrential downpour. "Mrs. Becker, I don't mean to be nosy, but you have a bit of an accent, I mean both of our parents have accents, too, and our mom says Canadian-y things that people don't understand such as calling the couch the chesterfield, and she says 'eh' a lot and progress is 'PRO-gress', and again is 'a-GAIN', so I don't mean this in any weird way but you sound almost like our dad, but his accent is still pretty strong and he mixes up his 'v's' with his 'w's' and 'th' is just 't' and he is Danish and I thought maybe you came from there or maybe from somewhere near there."

Meg paused for a moment, caught her breath and waited for Elke to answer.

"Oh, can you still hear it? You have a good ear. I have been trying for many years to lose this accent!" Elke took her last sip of tea and continued. "You see, I was born in Germany. Victor was born there as well. But we left when he was a little boy, so he doesn't remember it. I wanted him to know his heritage, though, so I have always spoken to him in both English and German. He is fluent in both." She stopped and smiled at that.

"Well, obviously he speaks English perfectly! How silly of me. Anyway, we both try to only speak English when others are around. Meg, there are still some people who don't like Germans. Even today, in 1972, some blame all of the Germans for the war." Elke looked down at the table before she uttered her next words. "Even those of us who also suffered the atrocities. There are people who just don't understand, nor do they realize, that they can't clump all Germans together. Some people cannot separate regular German citizens from the Nazis. We, I mean my family, well we were nothing like them." Elke looked down at her hands, for a moment, deep in thought. And then said softly, "And so, I try not to be too German."

The subtle change in Elke, a quiet sadness that seemed to surround her, prompted Meg to turn to her sister. Tapping her arm she said, "Hey, Sarah, we should get going. It's late." Sarah, taking the cue, got up and cleared their dishes. Giving Elke a hug, they thanked her and headed out the door.

Halfway through the woods, Sarah turned to her sister. "Hey, Meg, what was with the big rush? She was telling us so many things, things I really wanted to know."

"Sarah, she seemed incredibly sad while she was telling us about Germany. You know, she never really says much about herself. She does more listening. I guess maybe because I am always yammering away. Anyway, I thought it was better that we left right then. But I am curious. I wonder what happened to her during the war."

"Maybe we could ask her sometime."

"Maybe." But in her head Meg told herself that it might be best to leave alone a subject that was most likely too painful to discuss. "Anyway we had better get moving. Gotta throw these horsey clothes in the laundry before Mom gets home. I think she knows that we are up to something. Best not to give her anything more to be suspicious about."

"Yeah, Meg. Good plan. You know, your brilliant idea about offering to do the laundry on Sundays."

CHAPTER 7

ELKE

On an early November visit, Meg had all the symptoms of a nasty cold which worsened after they finished riding. Once in the kitchen, Elke brewed her a mug full of ginger root tea, adding honey, lemon and cinnamon. Meg, sipping the amber colored liquid, commented, "Mrs. Becker, that tea really was great and my throat even feels a bit better. Thank you. Maybe, if you have time one of these days, you could explain how all of this works? I mean, this tea, and that brew we made for Hudson and I guess other healing stuff, too."

"Of course! I would love to. I have time, right now, to start with a few things today. Just a few quick things, as I know you need to head home soon. Let's start right here in the kitchen, as there are so many examples right here. Then we can head out through the greenhouse on your way home."

Pointing to the ceiling, Elke indicated the bunches of fragrant dried herbs hanging near the stove area. "I love to use fresh herbs, when I can, but I dry them as well. Especially when I have more fresh herbs than I can use. All of the herbs drying in my kitchen do double duty. All add flavor in cooking or are made into teas, but they all also assist with healing. Oregano has a terrific flavor, and is used in Mediterranean cuisine. But it also has an antibiotic quality to it." She broke off a piece for them to smell.

Pulling down a pale green herb with grayish purple flowers, she explained, "This is lavender. Not only does it smell wonderful in sachets, it helps to calm and soothe and also helps people fall asleep. Here, take a bunch with you. Tuck some under your pillow tonight and you will see!" She then picked a piece off of a white and yellow flowered herb. "This is chamomile, which also helps to calm, and mixed with lavender it makes the perfect tea to sip before bedtime."

Elke then brought them into the greenhouse, proudly showing them her collection of plants. "This leafy plant is ginger. The root of this plant has all of the flavor, as well as the healing properties. Ginger tastes amazing, helps with the immune system and can also help to settle an upset stomach! I peel and cut the root to boil and make tea. Just like what....."

Stopping Elke midstream, Sarah burst out, "Oh, maybe that is why our mom always gives us ginger ale when our stomachs hurt. Actually, she lets it sit out, in a glass, so the bubbles disappear. I never thought of it being made from a root. I guess I always thought it was just soda that came in a bottle." Sarah was adorably excited by the discovery. Then, the realization that she had interrupted prompted her to add, "Oh, Mrs. Becker, I'm so sorry. You were talking."

"No harm done and that was more excitement on your part than anything! I have been talking way too much, anyway! I am so thrilled you are so interested! There is just so much to tell you about. Anyway, on a botanical level, a plant's hidden roots are extremely necessary. They bring the water and nourishment from the ground to the plant, and are often the best part! This next plant is turmeric. In this plant, it is also the root that helps the most. Turmeric helps with inflammation and swelling." Elke stopped for a moment, adding, "But a word of caution. Herbs and roots need to be used with care. Too much of anything is never good. And, if you are sick, you absolutely must see a doctor. But in the meantime, it is nice to know that Mother Nature has some natural ways to help us feel better, and to help us take care of ourselves."

Leading them to the other side of the greenhouse, she brought them to a collection of even more green leafy plants. "I grow all of these plants outside in the summer, and then bring them inside and replant them in pots when it gets too cold. That way I have lots of fresh vegetables year round. Carrots, parsnips, turnips, beets and radishes are called root vegetables. All possessing a lovely bit of greenery on top, the really great parts of them remain unseen. Until you dig them up! Often the best aspects of things are hidden and underground." Elke smiled and added softly, "Kind of like people. We never know how good they are until we look inside their soul and get to know them better. Sometimes the most important part of a person, just like root vegetables, is what is not broadcast overtly on the surface."

Elke stopped talking after she showed them the radish plant, hesitating. "But I don't want to give you too much all at once! Also, while we are on the subject of healing, I do want you both to know that I believe, with all of my heart, that the cures for all of the ailments in the world are hidden in nature. We just have to look harder for them. Long, long ago, people found cures, most of the time by accident, through the use of herbs and plants."

Picking up a piece of a dried and gray substance, she turned to the girls and explained, "For ages, people used to make a medicine from salicylate-rich plants, just like this one. This is called willow bark. When making this into a tea, it was discovered that it reduced fever and inflammation and that it also helped alleviate pain. We use this medicine today, but it is manufactured in plants now and sold in bottles. It's called aspirin. And that brings us to the perfect place to stop! You had better head home. It is getting late. Til next week!"

Once the girls eventually tore themselves away, Elke realized just how much she enjoyed their company. By absorbing information and taking it all in with enthusiasm, they were a pleasure to teach. But down deep she wished that she could do more than that for them, and for Sarah in particular. Each time they came for riding lessons, she tried to figure out the ways in which she could heal her. Probing questions were to no avail. Sarah wasn't taking the bait. Meg didn't help much either.

Knowing that something must have gone wrong for the injury not to have healed properly, she became more and more determined to figure out why. She wanted to fix it and she was certain she could do so. As the mid-November temperatures began to drop, Elke knew they wouldn't have much time left for riding lessons. Winter was on its way and the girls might not return again until spring. She would have to figure things out soon. In this case, with this injury of Sarah's, time alone would not necessarily be enough for healing. She had to hurry.

CHAPTER 8

THE FALL

One spontaneous moment on one memorable day gave Elke the opportunity to be able to assess Sarah's injury, and to finally begin the much needed healing process. Perhaps she had created the moment that ultimately occurred. Perhaps not. Still, when it happened, she was grateful for her little reptilian friend's assistance.

Sarah, riding Madison, was just coming around the back corner of the paddock when the horse suddenly lurched and rose up on her hind legs. A small garter snake had slithered across the sandy ground, directly in front of Madison's path. Holding on for dear life, Sarah called out, and then, strength sapped, simply just slipped off the back of the horse, landing right on her bottom. Turning around, the mare then nuzzled the girl with her soft muzzle, saying just how sorry she was in her very own equine way. Elke, already on the spot, had raced across to Sarah mere seconds after she saw Madison rear up. Quickly checking Sarah's pulse, Elke then started to examine her. Thankfully, Sarah appeared to have been uninjured from the fall itself. She was just stunned. But this situation presented the perfect excuse for Elke to see what else might be lurking beneath the surface.

"Sarah," Elke began. "Show me where it hurts. Point to where it has been hurting you since the accident. The car accident, not just now."

Whether it was because she felt truly comfortable with Elke, or that she was simply still a bit in shock, Sarah pointed to an area, just below her left knee, the same area that Elke had noticed as problematic, weeks earlier. "Here, Mrs. Becker. This was right where the bumper of the car hit. At least that is what the doctor told me."

"Sarah, I am just going to run my hand down the spot, if that is okay with you." Sarah nodded and Elke went forward. Rubbing down the girl's leg, she felt it, and saw it. Along the tibia, half way between the knee and the ankle, a violet glow radiated out to Elke, indicating to her that this area was damaged. It must never have healed properly. Thankfully, the light reassured her that her initial assessment was accurate. This was indeed not a new injury from the fall off of Madison's back. Elke could never have forgiven herself if that had been the case.

Meg, all throughout Elke's analysis, had been holding onto Sarah's hand. Elke turned to her and asked, "Meg, what happened to Sarah in the accident? Do you remember how her injury was diagnosed?"

Meg, a bit flustered, looked first at Sarah, waiting for approval. When Sarah nodded, she answered. "Mrs. Becker, the doctors told us that day, but I don't remember exactly. I think it was her tibia? Maybe the shaft. Is that a thing?"

"Hmm. Tibial shaft maybe." Elke pondered. "Did they say Tibial shaft fracture?"

"Yes, that was it. Pretty sure. Yeah, that sounds right." Meg continued. "Anyway, they put her in a cast, for months, and then she seemed fine. They said it might take time for complete healing, though. But I have always noticed that she favors that leg. A lot. And she said that it still hurts. More some days than others. At least she told me that. She never told our parents, though."

Meg looked down at the ground and it all tumbled out, things that Elke innately had already known. But it was still painfully poignant actually hearing the words coming directly and honestly from this young girl. Elke's heart ached for her.

"Mrs. Becker, it is not really good at home. Actually some days are pretty awful. It was better after the car accident, for a while. I mean it was less terrible then. For a while, my parents were happy. At least they seemed happy. But now, I don't know. Anyway Sarah didn't want to worry them. My parents I mean. They are in enough of a mess. Sarah is always so sweet, never wanting to be a bother. She kept thinking the pain would get better with time."

It appeared that there was more healing needed within this family than just the physical injuries. Emotional scars abounded for certain. But Elke needed to take care of this corporeal problem at hand before she could endeavor to delve into any of their spiritual needs.

Elke asked Sarah to lie down, her back on the ground, legs straight out in front of her. It made sense to leave the riding helmet on her head, as it offered protection from the hard ground underneath her. Gently pressing against the tissue around the tibia, she ascertained that clearly something was amiss. It had been almost two years since the car accident. That was a long time. Too long.

Keeping her assessment to herself, she made her decision. It didn't matter now if Meg and Sarah found out who she was. Or what she was. The girls had become special to her. She had to do something to help.

And so, she began her process. Her hand resting on the damaged portion of Sarah's leg, Elke looked up into the atmosphere and entered her healing trance. Calling on all that she knew, she drew on every one of her six senses, all of her healing powers, and asked for assistance, using words that neither girl would have understood. Sarah, eyes already squeezed shut, had fallen into a trance like slumber, so she would not have heard a thing. Meg was another issue. But hopefully Elke could explain things to the older sister. Later. In the meantime Meg just looked on in astonishment.

In what seemed like only a few seconds, it was all over. Sarah's eyes snapped open and she looked up at Elke, and then at Meg

"Wow. Wait. What just happened? Did I just fall off the horse? How clumsy of me." Sarah said in a soft and raspy voice that was hard to hear.

At that very moment, a shadow fell over them. Following the shape of the shadow and looking up, blinded a bit, they all saw its cause, contoured in the late morning sun.

"What on earth are you doing to my daughter!" The shape was now screaming at Elke's face. Grabbing her younger daughter's hands and yanking her to her feet, she said in an angry firm tone. "Girls. Come. Now."

Quickly unbuckling the helmet strap, she whipped the helmet from Sarah's head, throwing it to the ground next to Elke's feet. Elke jumped back just in time to miss the hit, and managed to at least make an attempt to defend the situation. "Mrs. Pedersen, she is fine."

Ignoring Elke, the woman said again to her daughters, even more emphatically."We are leaving. Now."

"But Mom! Why? This has been amazing. Mom, we know how to ride now!" Meg blurted out, all the while struggling to remove her helmet as quickly as possible, before her mother got to her, too.

Stunned, and unsure what to say or do, Elke watched, and also listened, as the woman led the way, daughters at her heels.

"You lied to me, Meg. You were supposed to be at church. You told me that was where you were going."

Meg defended them both. "We did go, Mom. We go every Sunday. But we go to early mass. Before you wake up."

Ruffled, but just momentarily, it took a beat for her to respond. "Still, you were wrong. You did not tell me about this very dangerous riding thing. Not that I would have approved anyway. It is your deception that I am angriest about. I am blaming you for this, Meg. You got your sister hurt. Once again. Just like the car accident. Had you only been paying attention...." Mrs. Pedersen spit out her tirade in a low and angry whisper as she herded the two girls away from the paddock. But Elke had heard most of it. The worst part anyway.

Just as they arrived at the edge of the woods, Mrs. Pedersen pivoted and returned back to address Elke. "I do not know who you are, or what you actually do, but this, this thing that you are doing or have done, is not right. It is not normal. I found the little map and directions. Today, in one of Meg's drawers. You must have made this for them, as it was in neither girls handwriting. I wondered where they were going all those Sunday mornings. They were supposed to be at church, and I have been curious because lately they have been coming home later and later. From what clearly was not church. Now I know why. I am furious with them, but even more disappointed…no, disappointed is not strong enough. I am livid and I am blaming you for all of this. They are never to come here again."

"Mrs. Pedersen, I am truly sorry. I thought, I mean they told me that you knew they were coming for riding lessons. Sarah had a fall. Just a little one. She is fine. I was just trying to help…" But Elke was talking to the wind. The woman had gone, the girls reluctantly trailing behind her. Glancing over their shoulders, for a last peak at Elke, they headed sadly and guiltily into the woods behind their mother.

CHAPTER 9

MEG

Several days after the incident at Elke's, Meg was finally able to sneak out of her house. It had been hard ever since that day, as her mother was watching them both like a hawk. They had been grounded, as a punishment for lying. Or rather they were in trouble for fact omission, for not actually telling their mother exactly what they were doing. But Meg had been patient, and she had figured out a day when her mother would be out of the house for quite a long time. She was prepared, and had planned accordingly. Making sure that Sarah would cover for her, she had also coordinated the ruse with Mary. They were supposedly working on a school project. Just in case the mother returned ahead of schedule.

Racing through the woods on the now very familiar path, she knew she had to use her limited time wisely. Out of breath, Meg reached the clearing and saw her friend near the paddock. Meg called out, "Mrs. Becker! Mrs. Becker!" Elke turned around to look at her quickly, but managed to avoid any eye contact. Turning around again, Elke headed to the cottage, walking at such a quick pace that she was almost running. Meg tried to catch up, bounding over the grass, following the woman with the white-blond braid bouncing against her back. But Elke was too far ahead and was at the cottage's back door when Meg called out one last time, "Mrs. Becker, please wait!"

She watched the woman enter the house, closing the door with a slam. Crushed, Meg felt as though she had been dismissed as a stranger. Reaching the door moments after it closed, she spoke through the impenetrable boundary, hoping Mrs. Becker might relent, and open the door. "Mrs. Becker. Please. I need to talk to you. I really, really hope that it isn't that you don't want to see me. I am assuming that you aren't allowed to see me. Even though that would be terrible, it hurts less that way. Believe me, I know my mom. I know she did something, or said something. Mrs. Becker, she often reacts like this. Actually she usually over reacts like this. A lot. I am so sorry."

The door remained closed. But Meg had come prepared. Tucking the corner of an envelop under the jamb of the door, she turned away and reluctantly headed back into the woods.

CHAPTER 10

THE LETTER

Torn, as she had wanted to see the girl, she knew that she had done what was best. She had only been following directions. The typed letter sitting open on the kitchen table had arrived two days earlier, and its words racing across the page were specific and direct. Under no circumstances was she, Elke Becker, to have any contact, whatsoever, with the two Pedersen girls. It sounded official, as though a lawyer had dictated it. Maybe one had. Or maybe the mother had had input from a person familiar with the law. Either way, the written words spoke firmly and forcefully. And so, on that day, even as Meg called to her, Elke knew she had to obey the directive. It went against every fiber of her being to be so cold to that lovely, kind girl. However she was also truly conflicted. She was a mother herself. Albeit with false perception, Mrs. Pedersen was simply thinking that her daughters had fallen under the spell of an evil influence. Elke herself would lay down and die to protect her own child. Understanding this other person's misunderstanding was making things even more difficult. She was simply trying to help the girls. It wasn't selfish, it was altruistic. But didn't she also get something out of it herself? Hadn't she enjoyed having them around? She wished she could make the other woman understand how harmless it all had been. But wait, she was clearly in the wrong herself. Why hadn't she been more insistent? Why hadn't she questioned the girls more closely? Down deep she had known, even on that first day, that they had not told their parents.

Talking out loud, now, she continued her self-arguing. "So yes, it is my fault. Clearly. No, it is not completely my fault. But wait, I was the adult in the room. So I am completely and totally to blame. Why am I fighting with myself? And why am I now sounding like Meg?"

Realizing she was getting nowhere, she stopped battling with her psyche, but not until she reprimanded herself for not having been more careful. Rarely did she let others in. This type of situation was exactly why she usually kept to herself. It was why she kept away from other people. The hurt could often be too great, once she opened up her heart to others. And so, she needed to get back to normal, and close up her heart once again. At least for the time being. It was time. Time to draw the shell around herself. Time to protect herself.

Heartbroken, she peered out through the parted curtain blocking the kitchen window and watched as Meg slowly worked her way back into the woods. Then she closed the curtain. Once she was certain Meg was no longer on the property, she reopened the door to pick up the envelop that she knew was waiting there. Tearing the seal, she took a few minutes to gather herself enough to read Meg's words. It was school-girl formal, written by hand, in clear and concise print.

November 30, 1972

Dear Mrs. Becker,

First of all, thank you so very much for letting Sarah and me ride Madison. Thank you for not only teaching us how to ride, but for showing us how to care for and love your horses. Also, thank you for all of the delicious cookies and cider and tea, and for healing Hudson. We also loved learning about the herbs. You are such a kind person. We will always remember our time at your special place.

But most of all, thank you for healing Sarah. I do not know exactly what you did, or how you did it, but her leg is so much better. She no longer has any pain. I think she just feels that it did really heal by itself. Finally. Don't worry, I will never let her know the truth. Especially about the really cool magical part!

I never told my parents about anything, even about what you did for Hudson. Actually neither one of us told them about that whole Hudson thing. We would have been in so much trouble. Anyway, Sarah still thinks it was just the herbs and the patting on his back. But I know now that it was so much more than just that. It was you and your special touch. All along.

I am not sure why my mother is angry with you. As usual, when I get into trouble or make her angry, she won't speak to me. It happens all the time, so I am used to it. Most of the time I don't even know what I have done wrong, but this time it is obvious. If I called that a relief, it might sound silly. But it is a kind of relief. At least I know where I stand.

So Sarah did tell me a little bit, as my mother never stops talking to her. Even when she herself gets into trouble, somehow it is me who is to blame. Sorry, I don't mean to pile up all of my family issues on you, but it is just that sometimes I need to talk about these things. Anyway, things in my house are rather lop sided. Sarah is always the angel, wearing the halo, especially since the accident. She can never do wrong. I am the baddie. The one with the pointy little horns on her head. It's okay. I'm super used to that, too.

Anyway, Sarah said that my mom thinks that you are some kind of witch and that you are dangerous. Sarah tried to convince her otherwise. Sarah really tried. But our mom doesn't want to discuss it. Ever.

Also, my mother was very firm saying that Sarah and I can never see you again. Ever.

I am trying to convince my parents, and mostly by that I mean my mother, that you are a kind and wonderful person. I am hoping that they, and by that I mean she, might let us return to your home, and maybe come ride again some day. She may come around. I will not give up.

I miss you and so does Sarah. Thank you. For everything.

Sincerely,

Meg Pedersen

PS It is really all our fault. We never should have lied about coming. We are both so sorry that we made such a terrible mess of things.

PSS Please give Madison a hug. And Scout, too.

PSSS Oh and say hi to Vic. From both of us.

PSSSS Sorry. I just wanted to add another PS for fun!

Laughing, and it was with much needed healing laughter, Elke realized that Meg wrote down words in the exact same manner as she spoke them. Reading her words, in a big and familiar tumble of thoughts, felt like they had actually just had a great visit. For that she was grateful. After carefully folding up the letter, she tucked it into the kitchen drawer. That letter was a keeper, for sure. She was really going to miss that girl. Both of the girls, actually, but Meg the most. Somehow that girl had completely stolen her heart.

CHAPTER 11

ELKE

It was a long and bitter winter. Busy as always, Elke plodded through the shorter colder days. From dawn until late at night she was consistently occupied with her job at the hospital, maintaining her home, and taking care of the animals. Even though her son was rather self-sufficient, she took care of Victor, too. Plaguing her thoughts daily, though, were the unresolved issues with the Pedersen family. Knowing that the girls felt guilty, she shared that same guilt. Fearing that they must have gotten into a lot of trouble, even more than Meg had alluded to, she continued to blame herself for the entire situation.

She had not dealt with things thoroughly, from the get-go. In her heart she knew it all needed to be addressed. If only there were a way to explain. Perhaps she could get through to the mother by speaking directly to her. Maybe the other woman would understand everything if she knew why things were the way they were. The devil on her shoulder wanted her to tell the woman everything, to get it all out in the open. But then the angel on the other shoulder stopped her from the insanity that would ensue should that conversation occur. If she were to divulge the part she kept most private it would prove most detrimental. Because, for certain, if she had even broached the subject of her healing "powers", they would have her taken away. To the nearest institution.

Knowing how unfathomable what she did would appear to outsiders, if they were to discover it, Elke just kept is self contained. But there was more, more than just the gift of being able to heal. Not only was she a healer, she was also an empath. The empath in her definitely helped in the healing, but it made the healings even more difficult for her. Healings took a toll on her mind, and on her body. She physically and emotionally took on and felt the pain and illness of others. Most people could never even begin to understand that such a thing could even occur. Therefore they were ignorant of the fact that Elke was actually absorbing their pain. Unsuspecting, they would spontaneously feel better, never realizing that their problem had simply shifted over. Into Elke.

But it wasn't actually a simple thing, this shifting from one person to another. Therefore it was best to keep her exposure to a minimum. In order to not take on too much, she would pick and choose the when and where of the healings that she undertook. By keeping to herself at home, it was really only the animals who were her "patients." Sometimes it was her son. Work, though, was another issue. She did what she could while working at the hospital. Most of the time she left situations in the hands of the doctors, but on occasion she would see a hopeless situation in a patient, and she would then assist in bringing about a healing. Quietly walking away afterwards, she would let no one ever know that the patient's improvement had actually been her. All along. So now, this current dilemma with the Pedersens needed a fix, although this was far different from her normal healings. Based on not only what she had observed, but through conversations with the girls, things were not right in the household. Adding to the mess that already existed, what she had done had not helped matters. It was time to take control of things, not only for the sake of the girls but also for her own health and well-being. It was eating away at her.

And so, one dark and chilly winter evening, she sat down and composed a heartfelt letter. A letter assuming all responsibility. A letter requesting forgiveness, not for her own deeds, but for the girls' deeds which had been falsely misinterpreted as misdeeds.

One afternoon in early March, she lied to her boss, just a little bit, saying that she had an appointment. It wasn't really a lie. She did have a meeting. Only the person with whom she had that meeting wasn't yet aware of it. Leaving the hospital just after lunchtime, she headed back north to Beauville, the letter ready and tucked into an envelop, resting on the dashboard.

C H A P T E R   1 2

THE ENCOUNTER

Spending very little time in the actual town center due to her self contained living situation, Elke made her visits into Beauville short and specific. Ever since she had moved to the woods outside of town years earlier, she had kept a low profile. Since the aspects of her life were too hard to explain, it was easier if she kept herself far away from inquisitive town folk.

Working twenty-five miles away also kept things removed. Victor attended school in Beauville, but that was the only connection. That and paying taxes. Avoiding school functions, other than to attend her son's soccer games, Elke was basically an outsider. She shopped and ran most of her errands on her way home from work. So she wasn't totally familiar with the exact layout of the entire town, and was a bit apprehensive as she pulled in that afternoon.

Working her way along the eastern side of the lake, she finally found the street for which she searched. Lakeview Terrace. It was, indeed, as the girls had told her, on a hill lined with pines, overlooking the lake. The lake around which Beauville existed. Elke had already checked the phone book for the house number, and so she pulled her two-tone, blue and white 1956 Roadmaster into the driveway. Her old but trusty Buick. She had bought it used, after saving for ages, two years after she had arrived in the States. Her first big purchase on her own. It was a tank of a vehicle, but it functioned well. And it started every time.

She turned off the engine, took a deep breath and gathered her emotional strength. Tentatively, she headed up the walkway. Ringing the doorbell, she waited patiently and uneasily. It was one-thirty in the afternoon. The girls would still be at school. Mr. Pedersen, as the girls had told her, commuted by train every weekday to New York City and got home late in the evening. It should be only Mrs. Pedersen at home. Just the person she needed to see.

"What are you doing here?" queried the tall brunette, peeking her head around the red door, opened just enough.

"Mrs. Pedersen, please, I just want to explain." Elke beseeched.

"I asked around about you, Mrs. Becker. Everyone in town says that you are that strange loner who lives up on the hill in the middle of the woods with all those animals like some fairy-tale witch. And for some bizarre reason, you have decided to befriend, oh and also bewitch my two daughters."

"Mrs. Pedersen I am not a witch nor was it my intention to do anything untoward with your daughters. I am, as you might have heard, a healer and I am in addition, a trained nurse. Well at least I was a trained nurse in my home country, as they couldn't get my actual educational records from...." But Mrs. Pedersen never heard a word. She had already slammed the door shut. Prepared for the worst, as Elke had assumed in advance that the woman would not want to speak to her, she dropped her envelop through the mail slot in the middle of the red door.

As quick as it had been, Elke had gleaned from the encounter something completely unexpected. Instead of being angered by the woman's rapid dismissal, she found herself awash in pity for her. Taken aback, she worked her way back to her car and sat there, for a moment, collecting herself to keep her own emotions in check. Taking a calming deep breath, she pulled out of the drive and headed back towards town.

To clear her head, and perhaps needing to shake off some of the cloak of sadness that enshrouded her, she found herself driving aimlessly around the lake. Eventually ending up at the snow covered beachfront, she turned off her engine. She needed a walk.

Switching out her shoes for her rubber boots in the trunk, she set out. Trudging through the slushy snow covering the still frozen sand, thoughts milled through her brain. This woman, this beautiful, totally put-together woman was not at all whom she appeared to be. There was indeed something much more going on, something lurking down deeper than her immediate surface projected. Elke didn't know how to process it, any of it, especially not at that time.

CHAPTER 13

BEAUVILLE

Standing at the waters edge for ages that afternoon, Elke realized what a special place her little town really was. Research-
ing it thoroughly before she had even moved there, the reasons
she had come were now right in front of her, reaffirming that
decision. Beauville, originally two words, Beau Ville, beautiful
town, had been aptly named by a small group of founders from
France in 1775. During the mid-nineteenth century the town
became a summer retreat for New York City dwellers. Cottag-
es, summer homes and small hotels sprang up all over the area.
Over time, people began to convert the homes to year-round
dwellings and the population expanded significantly.

Early on, town planners managed to maintain the orig-
inal idyllic setting. By establishing ground rules, retail stores
and other businesses were allocated a specific area facing one
section of the lake. Charming storefronts on Main Street were
country style, with an old fashioned cinema and two waterfront

restaurants, with docks on the water for boats to park. The town diner, with checkerboard flooring and an ice cream counter, also had a vintage soda fountain and a jukebox in the corner. A small park with a gazebo kept the center of the town dedicated to foot traffic only.

As the local high school was only a five minute walk from the town center, teens spent their afternoons there, hanging out at the various establishments. The diner, pizza parlor and baker's cafe were the best spots. That was until summertime arrived. Once the weather turned warmer, everything shifted to the waterfront.

The beach, where she was standing at the moment, was cordoned off with long wooden docks, indicating and protecting the boundaries of the swimming area from the boating areas. Small sail boats and canoes would be docked nearby as soon as the weather permitted. The remainder of the waterfront was conserved town land. One could not build homes on the lake, but houses were dotted all along the road that circled the waterfront, providing stunning views from their high perches on the surrounding hills.

Beauville was on the Harlem line, and an easy commute from its quaint stone train station to Grand Central. Only fifty miles north of New York City, the town was more than just a bedroom community. It was often a tourist stopover, especially in the autumn when the leaves displayed their stunning palette of red, rust and yellow. Reflections on the lake were breathtaking, all year long.

Winter in Beauville was a Currier and Ives etching. Whispering winds relieved snow laden willows, swirling white laced tendrils onto the ice. Mittened skaters, within the confines of snow shoveled ovals, practiced their skills and performed intricate hockey maneuvers. Bundled up sledders hiked up the hill to the north, trailing sleds and toboggans behind them. Gliding gleefully down, they ended their run, smoothly sliding across the frozen waters. Hurrying back, they would repeat the descents over and over again.

Graying snow now dusted the shoreline as Elke looked out over its expanse. Time had eroded, and she had completely lost track of just how long she had been standing there, letting the surrounding beauty calm her racing mind. An afternoon breeze had kicked in and with it came a sense of relief, her head finally cleared. Buttoning up her coat, as the air had cooled significantly, she headed back to her old Buick. She vowed to herself to take greater advantage of this incredible place more often in the future. Maybe she should sequester herself less and spend more time at the water's edge.

Easing her way slowly back down main street, she caught sight of a sign. "Beauville Dance Academy," where Meg and Sarah took classes. And so, a bit trepidatiously, Elke pulled into the little parking lot reserved for the studio. It took a few minutes to get up the nerve, but she turned off the engine and ventured out of her car, towards the building's entryway. Stopping abruptly, she began a debate with her conscience.

"They might not even be there yet. School has just let out. Go ahead, just go on in. You aren't even sure which days they attend anyway. This probably isn't one of their days. Besides, you just want to see where they dance. No. Don't mess with this. You know it isn't smart to do this. This is why you live in the woods. Keep to yourself, don't let others in. It is way too complicated... But it would be lovely to just say hello. Just a simple hello couldn't hurt. If they are even there." Once again, she was having an argument with herself. No one was winning. "Make up your mind, Elke. Okay. Here I go. I am going in." Self-assured, almost, she moved forward. Still a bit hesitant, as though she were walking through tacky, freshly poured cement she reached the studio door. Since it was ajar, she trepidatiously headed in. The lobby was filled with photographs on the walls, pictures showing dancers of all ages in various costumes. There were several sections labeled into categories which she assumed must be different ballets. Ignorant of ballet, the titles meant nothing to her. But Nutcracker, now that one was one she knew. Well, sort of. Meg had told her all about the Nutcracker. It was a Christmas ballet, one that they were in annually, taking on different parts each year. Elke spotted a few photos of both Pedersen girls, costumed and wearing stage make-up and looking so grown up.

Feeling someone behind her, she turned around and found herself caught up in a tight bear hug. "Mrs. Becker! It is you! I can't believe it! It really is you!" Meg pulled back from the hug, and was standing side by side next to another girl, several inches shorter than she was. Both girls were dressed in school clothes, each holding a leotard, tights and what Elke figured must be the pointe shoes that Meg had described. Pale pink, and ribboned. They looked so pretty, but supposedly they were those cruel culprits that brought on countless blisters, calluses and pain. Pointe work was that necessary skill that Meg had explained she needed to master in order to advance in her levels at the school.

Realizing she had been lost in thought, Elke snapped out of her head and answered Meg. "Oh, forgive me. Caught up in my mind. Hi Meg! It is just lovely to see you! I was in the neighborhood, and saw the studio and I thought I might just pop in." Elke smiled, a bit crookedly as she wasn't sure whether or not she should tell the truth about where she had just been earlier.

Meg added, still smiling,"I still just can't believe you are actually here! Oops, I am being so rude. Mrs. Becker, I want you to meet someone. This is Mary. She is my best friend, and she is also the best dancer in the studio!"

"Hi! Wow, finally, I get to meet you! Meg has told me so much about you, Mrs. Becker! And she is way too nice and complimentary about me!" Mary then turned to Meg. "We have to hurry and change, Meg. Class starts in five minutes!"

"Please stay and watch, Mrs. Becker!" Meg said over her shoulder as she turned to head towards the changing room. "Sarah is here, too! She is already in her class, in the room next to mine. She will want to see you after her class ends, I am sure!"

Elke stood, transfixed, watching the dance classes from the two doorways. She alternated back and forth, trying to observe both, trying not to miss anything. First, Meg's class, and then Sarah's. Then she repeated the pattern. They were lovely to watch. Indeed she did see what Meg meant about Mary. Even though she did not know much about dance, there was something incredible about that young girl. She was stunning. Mesmerizing.

Both classes ended at the same time, and as soon as Sarah saw Elke she raced to greet her friend in a sweaty hug. "We have missed you, Mrs. Becker. How are Madison and Scout?"

"They are good, but they miss you as well. And I trust Hudson is doing well?" Sarah nodded, smiling.

Meg had joined them after removing her pointe shoes. Elke turned to both girls, "I can't stay here. Your parents won't be happy about this."

"You mean our mother. Good thing you came when you did. She had just dropped us, so you missed her. Anyway, yeah, she finally told me everything that she said to you in that letter she mailed to you. Once she decided I was worthy of being spoken to again, she figured that I may as well know what she did." Meg grabbed Elke's hand. "We will find a way to smooth this over. I am sorry."

"Oh, Meg, don't be sorry. It was my fault. I should have been more insistent that your parents knew you were coming for riding lessons. I was just so happy to have you there!" Elke pulled back, and started to head towards the door, but Sarah grabbed her in a hug before she could escape.

"We really want to come back!"

"Sarah, I am not so sure that is a good thing. Listen, I don't blame her. She is your mother and she worries about you." Not sure if she should tell them, she hesitated, but then realized that she should prepare them. Just in case the mother said something later. "Anyway, I stopped by earlier to talk to her, to apologize. It wasn't…" She stopped herself at that point. No need to let the girls hear anything negative. Things were already negative enough. Just keeping it vague, she finished her sentence. "…a good time for her to see me. Anyway, I left her a note, though. As you, Meg, did for me back in the fall. Thank you for that, by the way." She gave the girls one last hug. "I wanted to also apologize to you two as well. Because I should have been more forthright. I am sorry that you both got into so much trouble. But I do need to get going now. It is late."

With that, she turned around abruptly. Once back in her car, she kicked herself for telling them that she had been to see their mother. She should have just kept quiet. Or, better yet, she should not have gone to the studio at all. But, then again, it had been so nice seeing them. It was a relief. Both girls seemed so happy, not only happy to see her, but happy in general. That was a good thing. She smiled to herself as she headed home.

CHAPTER 14

EVELYN

Early April. The crocuses were in full bloom, and the daffo-dils were just beginning to open their golden faces, smiling up at the warm spring sun. Evelyn was pulling up some of the early weeds starting to sprout around the lilac trees. It was a diversion, keeping herself physically busy so that her mind didn't explode. What was that woman thinking? Allowing perfect strangers to ride horses. Without seeking parental permission. Such a dan-gerous, reckless thing. What if Sarah had gotten hurt again? It was all completely inexcusable. Evelyn had almost put the whole incident away. Until it reared its ugly head again yester-day. Why did that woman go ahead and so blatantly disobey the directive? It had been so very clear, that letter.

It was infuriating. That woman was completely infuriating.

Gathering the bundle of weeds, she headed across the street and tossed them into the woods. And there it was. The path. Right there in front of her. The path to that woman's house. On an impulse, and mostly subconsciously, she started heading up, not really thinking about what she was doing or where she was going. Just walking. It didn't take long, this uphill hike through the woods. There was so much to distract her, making the trek seem to be even shorter. Trees beginning to burst into full foliage loomed overhead and chipmunks darted nearby, tails up, crunching their way through the leaves. Absorbed by the visual diversion of the forest's beauty, she had arrived at the clearing without realizing how far she had actually wandered. Stopping in her tracks, she was about to turn back and head home. But then she saw her.

Elke Becker. That annoyingly beautiful blond was now on horseback, expertly guiding a dark brown mount in circles around the paddock. Looking relatively tiny upon that giant animal, she was so much in control, so confident and so positively proficient. It was extremely aggravating. She could hear her, giving commands to the horse, in some unrecognizable language. German perhaps. Even though Evelyn was aggravated, something about the vision was completely riveting. Hidden now, tucked behind a tree and unseen, she couldn't help herself from staring. She knew she should leave before being noticed, but she couldn't. Once the anger rose up from her gut, she finally was motivated to move forward.

Heading over to the paddock, she then simply stood there, leaning against the fence, utterly silent. Waiting. The woman circled around once more and spotted her. Arriving near Evelyn, she brought the horse wordlessly to a stop, a few feet away. With the fencing as a separation, there was a natural and necessary boundary lying between them.

Looking down from her perch, Elke spoke cooly but cordially. "Good afternoon, Mrs…"

"I am not entirely sure who you think you are, Mrs. Becker. And what you have done is inexcusable. My youngest daughter Sarah is sweet and kind but naive and easily corrupted, most often due to the antics of her big sister. This time, though, it is you who are causing the trouble in my family. You were told to stay away from my two daughters, but you did not. Sarah told me, yesterday, by accident, as I am sure she was trying for weeks to keep it quiet. It spilled out as she cannot lie to me. She told me that you went to the studio that day in March, the day after you came to see me. I did read your letter, by the way, but no, I will not forgive you. Nor will I forgive the girls."

"Mrs. Pedersen......"

But Evelyn had already turned around, and was heading back down the path towards the woods.

CHAPTER 15

MEG

Digging her toes deeply into the sand, she pulled the extra towel over her legs to further protect them from the burning overhead rays. Even though it was late afternoon, there was no stopping the effect of the sun on her skin. Adjusting the brim of her hat, she looked over at her friend, lying face down and soaking up all of the available remaining rays.

"You know I really should hate you!" She said this to herself, but not really.

"Well you don't really hate me now, do you?" It was a statement more than a query, muffled due to the fact that Mary's face was currently buried in her towel.

"Wait. Are you awake?" Meg hopefully turned down the volume of the transistor radio blaring beside her.

"No. I am just talking in my sleep."

"Come on, Mary. I'm bored."

Rolling over she looked up at Meg with her hand on her forehead, shielding her brown eyes from the glare. "You look like a hot dog in a bun."

"An ounce of prevention, a pound of less sunburn." She traced a line from one freckle to the next, saying, "I had hope, once upon a time, that all of these charming freckles would just decide to connect and merge into one seamless and gorgeous tan, but it never did work! Lord knows that I have tried. One burn after the other. It is hopeless. I have now, at the wise and ancient age of fourteen, finally given up." Meg rearranged the towel again, illustrating her point. "Glad you are awake."

"Didn't have much of a choice, now did I?" Sitting up, she looked with concern at her best friend. "There clearly is no stopping you once you want to talk. That we all know for certain. Okay. What is rattling all around that brain of yours? Come on. Out with it. I am all ears."

Meg started, in her usual way, to explain. All at once. "Okay. Here it is. I really wish I didn't have to go to the cottage this year. But mom is all squirmy and wants to go, so go we must. I really wish I could just hang out with you every day at the beach. This beach. Silly really. We live here, right near this beautiful lake. A lake complete with the perfect beach. Then we pack up our car like we are being exiled, drive ten hours, to another country no less, to go and live in a little cottage on another lake, with sort of a beach. A rocky one, though. They are both, still, just bodies of water."

"Well, Beauville Lake, as nice as it is, isn't quite exactly the Georgian Bay. But, yeah I hate when you go. It is rather dull around here without you." And smiling, with a wink, Mary added, "I do sleep a bit more, though."

"Sleep is overrated. Mary, can you believe we are finally going to be in High School in a little bit. High School! Did you ever imagine we would ever really get there? I keep wondering if I am going to run into Vic. Do you think that he might just remember me? Even if he does, he most likely won't pay attention to me, though. He will be a Junior and I will be just a lowly Freshman."

"Stranger things have happened, Meg. You never know. Maybe it will be the romance of the century."

"Yeah right. Sure. Anyway, I need a good story right about now. To cheer me up." She gave Mary her puppy-dog eyes, knowing full well that her friend would comply with her request. "Can you tell me the one about when your parents met again? It is the best love story ever. So almost unbelievable, yet it is real!"

"Yeah, sure. It has only been about a month since I last told it to you. That might just be a record." Mary grinned at her friend and began."Okay. You can probably chime in, as you know it almost better than me at this point. Right. So it is World War II and my mom is a nurse. My dad is in the army. He gets fatally wounded, or at least that is what they all thought."

"And he was in a deep dark coma, and your mother was his nurse and she never gave up on him!" Meg eagerly chimed in, as requested.

"Correct. Weeks went by and my mother sat by his side, holding his hand, wiping his brow, and talking to him as if he were alive."

"Then finally, one day, he woke up! Just like Sleeping Beauty. But in reverse." Meg's turn.

Mary went on, clarifying. "Sort of. I guess. Minus the whole royalty thing and the kiss and all. Oh and it wasn't like a hundred year sleep, either. Anyway, when my mother saw his eyes opened she called out for the doctor. But my dad then stopped her, grabbed her hand and looked at her. Right into her eyes, and he saw that she had tears streaming down her face and he finally spoke and said…."

Mary paused because she knew that Meg would want to say her favorite part. "He said: 'Thank you for never giving up on me. I heard everything. All those stories that you were telling me, the whole time. I am pretty sure that I am in love with you!' Or something like that. Then they married and lived happily ever after. The most perfect, most romantic story ever. Oh, Mary, I really do want the exact same thing! My own perfect love story! My very own fairytale ending."

CHAPTER 16

ELKE

Elke went back on her promise to herself to spend more time in town. Hesitating now, she only went in when an emergency situation warranted it, ever since her last trip there had caused such an issue. Worried that she might just run into Meg's mother, she took care of errands and such in other places. However, she was low on supplies for the barn and needed to pop into the local feed and grain store to place an order. So she bit the bullet and headed to the town center.

On her way home, she passed the dance studio. Magnetically drawn to the place, she had a passing, yet inane thought that she should just pop her head inside. Just for a peek. A sign outside indicated that there was a summer dance program, that week. Maybe the girls would be there. Without thinking, she pulled her car into a spot in front of the building. No. Mrs. Pedersen would not take kindly to this, should she get wind of it. Elke knew, somehow, that she would indeed find out. Second thoughts collided with her conscience, and she snapped to attention. As she shifted her car into reverse, she heard a familiar voice through the opened passenger door window.

"Aren't you Mrs. Becker?"A lovely young lady, dark brown hair in a bun, was heading toward the studio. "Hi! I am Mary, Meg's friend."

Elke stopped the car and applied the brake. "Oh, my goodness, yes. I am Mrs. Becker. And I do remember meeting you, and watching you dance!" And, pausing, for a beat, she asked the next question. "Are Meg and Sarah taking summer classes?"

"Oh, no. They are actually at their cottage in Canada. They go for most of the summer."

Partly disappointed, partly relieved as she feared the mother's wrath, Elke said to the young girl, "So sorry I have missed them, but do give them my best when you next see them."

"I will, Mrs. Becker. They really do miss you."

"I feel the same." Elke then backed her car out and headed home.

CHAPTER 17

First Day

Stepping out of the car, she hits the lock and shuts the door, right before she realizes that she has completely forgotten to get dressed that morning. She is, in fact, stark naked. Wearing not even a stitch of clothing, she is standing in a busy parking lot, packed with cars. Frantically grabbing the door handle which somehow will not open, mostly because it is, of course, locked, she peers in, only to see a shiny pile of keys on the seat.

Waking up in a sweat, she looked down to see that she was indeed not naked, but clad in pajamas and thankfully no longer in the parking lot. But she had slept through her alarm clock and if she didn't hustle she would be late for school. The first day of High School.

Thankfully she wasn't too late to catch up with Mary, who was herself running a little bit late, and they both miraculously arrived at the high school on time. Meg managed to get through the first few periods of the day unscathed, mainly because she was following the hordes of other confused freshmen as they wandered through the building. But third period was a problem. No one she knew had this next class.

Clutching the map of the floor plan, trying to figure out how to get there within the next two minutes, she felt her heart pound. It was her worst recurring nightmare, getting lost and being late for class. Well, it was her second worst nightmare. She had already had her first worst nightmare earlier that morning.

Once a year, that naked dream would rear its ugly head. Usually in September, it would occur a night or two before the school year began. It never varied. Figuring that there must be some logical and/or psychological interpretation which might explain it, she had gone to the library to be sure. Hoping it didn't mean she had gone nutty, or had somehow become possessed, she knew she had to find the reason for this possible madness. A creature of ever-present curiosity, she researched it all. Every aspect. Although it didn't help stop the recurrence, she did learn that dreams like that happened for a reason. The naked one meant one was revealed and vulnerable. Either that or one was finally freed from a burden. Bared to the world. Something like that. Nothing really concrete from the dream experts. Just speculation really. She hadn't lost her mind, as many people had this type of dream, so she was somewhat reassured. However, no matter what, the nightmares were awful and they left her shaking when she awoke. Which was exactly how she felt at that very moment while racing through the hallway.

Looking alternately at the map and then the class schedule frantically, she was not exactly paying attention to what lay in front of her. Almost at full tilt, she crashed directly into a poor and unsuspecting soul. Books and papers scattered everywhere.

"Well, hello there!" Following the direction of the voice above her, she looked up and found her eyes focused on the bluest eyes she had ever seen. Those eyes. Why do I know those eyes? How on earth could they actually be that color? Does that color even exist in nature? Were they the color of the ocean? Or of the sky? Or both? So lost in her contemplation she was late-out-of-the-gate in realizing that she was, at the moment, plastered against a very tall and very good looking blond. Once reality hit, a hot red blush oozed from the base of her neck and worked its way up through her face, scorching its way straight up to her astonished eye brows.

Seemingly void of all logical thought, she managed to merge together the only two words that came to her brain at the moment. "Vic….Hi…."

Lingering a millisecond too long, her brain finally sent the message to her physical self that she had taken way too long in removing her body from its current state. Carefully, she peeled herself away. Hopefully before anyone else noticed. The whole vision just might have been misconstrued as a rather romantic embrace had it been under any other circumstance.

In her feeble attempt to gather even a remote modicum of dignity, she took a deep breath and managed to utter a few intelligible words. "I can't find it. I mean I can't find Biology. I mean the class, not actual biology…"Another blush flowed through her as he raised his left eyebrow, and looked down into her eyes. "I mean the lab. Room 113…."

"It is a little tricky. Here, just turn right down that hall and then tuck into that little side hallway." He pointed it out, and then, seeing her baffled look, changed his mind. "Wait. I can show you." He leaned down and gathered her books and papers, organizing them into a manageable pile. "Follow me." And he walked her towards the classroom. Meg, now empty-armed, followed a step behind him in a robotic trance. They arrived just seconds before the bell. He handed her the books, and then turned to leave.

Common courtesy superseded terror, and she managed to mutter, "Thanks so much."And then, miraculously, there was actually some additional brain function. She gasped, "Oh no! What about you? You will be late for your class now. Oh and now me too! So sorry. Gotta go." But he was already gone. She slipped quickly into the room before she would be marked late. Distracted, Meg managed to bumble through the Bio class, jotting down the year's expectations and upcoming assignments as thankfully, that rote task required little actual thought. The bell rang, jarring her to attention. Wondering why her usually pretty together student-self was so disjointed, she absentmindedly gathered her notebook and textbooks into an atypically disorganized pile and headed out the door. Stopping and leaning against the lockers that flanked the hallway, she consulted her map. She was so absorbed in utter concentration that she gasped when she heard his voice once more.

"Let me guess. You aren't sure where you need to go. Once again." Victor came up beside her, looked over her shoulder and glanced quickly at the schedule in her hand. Her blush started all over again, hotter this time. What a vision she must be, her copper penny hair clashing with her now beet-red freckled skin, green eyes most likely popping.

"Oh. This one is easy. It's your lunch period. Unfortunately you got stuck with the earliest lunch. Happens to freshmen all the time. I have a free period next. I can hang with you." He had laid his hand companionably on her shoulder. She froze.

Words, at least a few, formed in her head again. Thankfully almost in sentence form. But translating them into an actual formulation of speech was not so simple. "Thanks... so sorry... Middle School was so easy... All one floor... I just need to get used to this."

"By the way, you look great in glasses." Victor turned and looked directly into her emerald eyes. "I have never seen you in them. You look smart. Well, I know you are smart. Honors Bio as a freshmen. Wow, I am impressed." Flustered, she dropped her books. Again.

He gathered up the books. Again. "Listen, I was supposed to be looking for you anyway. Even before you crashed into me." He smiled the warmest smile, looking at her sideways as he handed the books back to her, carefully tucking them back into the crook of her now petrified arms. "My mom asked me to check on you. She figured you would be just getting used to High School. She misses you and Sarah."

For some inane reason, she couldn't speak. She did discover though, that she had a bit of muscle control remaining. So she just nodded.

He took the lead. "Okay. Let's head to the cafeteria for your lunch."

They placed their books on an empty table, and grabbed trays, heading over to the food selection. It all looked rather gray and drab and dreadful. Victor pointed out the food that most likely wouldn't kill them, and they managed to find a few things that appeared to be remotely edible. She was glad that they were chewing and eating so that she didn't really have to talk. Struggling with the loss of basic verbal ability, there was little chance of managing to sound even remotely coherent. All she could do was nod and smile as Victor talked about life at Beauville High.

He sat with her for a few minutes after they finished eating, and then stood to leave.

"I have to head out. Your next class is down that hall to the left." He pointed through the crowded room towards one of the exits. As he took a few steps away, he turned back to her and added, "And hey. There is a practice soccer game at four today. She is coming. My mom I mean. Maybe you could come, too?"

Finally some words appeared in her head, and she could read them, and see them, as if they were written in chalk on the board. They managed to work their way to her mouth where she was actually able to execute the sounds that those words should make. However, much to her chagrin, the words ended up sounding as stiff and precise as if spoken by an ancient schoolmarm. "Oh, Vic, I would love that. I will be there. Most certainly." He smiled, waved and headed to the door. Hating her idiotic self, she banged her forehead with her palm, "Why do I do this?"And then she realized she had a conflict in the afternoon and she called out, too late, into the noisy, echoey room. "Oh no! I have band after school. Wait. It ends at 4:30. I could come over after that…..maybe."

She realized she was stammering again. Essentially to herself as he was out of earshot.

CHAPTER 18

MEG

Later that afternoon, immediately after band practice, she raced out of the school building. But this time she had prepared herself. Starting up a conversations with one of the sophomore girls in the clarinet section whom she had remembered from middle school, she discovered where the soccer field was located. So she knew she was heading in the right direction. She dreaded getting lost again. And she couldn't wait to see Mrs. Becker. Or maybe it was that she couldn't wait to see Vic. Watching him play soccer wouldn't be such a bad thing, now would it? Maybe if he looked as incredible on the soccer field as he had on horseback..... Wait. Stop. Get a hold of yourself. He is just being nice. Because of his mom. Now you are overreacting and you are thinking things through, way, way too much. Suddenly she realized that not only did her speech stammer when she was nervous, her brain was now following suit. Why was she such a mess? What the heck was wrong with her?

Just before skidding into the side of the hill overlooking the field, she broke her run into an optimistically nonchalant saunter. Well, almost nonchalant. Her stomach was doing flips and she was convinced people could actually see it popping through her shirt as it rolled over and over. Pushing her hair out of her eyes, she attempted to pull herself together, hoping she would appear like the reasonable facsimile of a calm person.

Muttering to herself, something she was doing more and more lately, she made a stab at trying to convince herself to actually get it together. "Look steady, now, Meg. Or at least pretend that you are put together." Covering her eyes to shield them from the glaring afternoon sun, she scanned the packed bleachers trying to locate a seat. One spot. There, kind of on the side, unobtrusively two rows in. "Don't look too eager, now Meg." Dear Lord, she needed to stop this inner monologue.

Settling herself in on the aluminum bench, she looked through the crowd for a familiar face. It was the Varsity game, so most of the onlookers were upperclassmen. So she knew no one. Then, disappointed, she noticed Mrs. Becker wasn't there either. Maybe she would come later.

Busying herself, Meg focused all of her attention on the game, trying to relate the sport to known entities. She sort of understood soccer. They played it once in a while during gym class. Goals. Kind of like in hockey. Dribbling with out-turned feet, wow, kind of like a bad first position in ballet. But the players used no hands, well except for the goalie. For some reason he could use his hands. And then they did those head butts. That had to hurt. She was getting it. Mostly.

The best part, though, despite her general ignorance, was watching Vic play. He handled the white and black ball expertly, and made two goals before the game ended in a tie. That much she could figure out. After the match, she saw him say goodbye to his teammates, grab his gear and start to head over to where Meg was still sitting, waiting. For what she was not entirely certain. But she had hoped he might come and say hello, so she had decided to stay put.

"Meg, I'm sorry. Not sure why she didn't get here. She sometimes has to stay late at work." Victor sat down on the bleacher bench and organized his clothes and books into a manageable bundle. He was sitting a few inches away from her, and that familiar blush was making a nasty habit of itself. Again. She felt it creep slowly, even more slowly this time. Oozing up her neck and onto her face. That hot red lava-like flow was becoming the norm.

Words came. Thankfully. However they all tumbled out in a breathless stream of a run-on sentence. Standard fare for Meg, so nothing new. "It's okay maybe next time and please tell her I said hello but actually I liked watching the game as it looks like fun and you are really good but I need to head home now and thanks again for asking me to come." She collected her things and stood up abruptly, but a bit too abruptly, banging her leg against the bleacher. Hard. Wincing, but trying with all her might to pretend that it hadn't actually happened, she bravely held in the urge to yell "ouch" rather loudly. However, since there was no mistaking the rather loud sound it had just made, nor was there any way to hide the pained wince on her face, Vic had indeed noticed. "Hey Meg, are you okay? You hit that leg pretty hard."

Mortified, she sucked in her breath and managed to wheeze out between her teeth, "Yup I am just fine but I have to go and I don't live really far away and I should start walking now as it is getting super late."

"I usually take the late bus home after the games, but it is really nice out, and I think I will walk, too. Can I join you, at least part way?"

Unable to process any verbal answer whatsoever, she just nodded and smiled, a bit crookedly and nervously. They then headed across the field, Meg hobbling quite a bit. Working their way down the hill towards the town center, he kindly stopped often to let her catch up. Vic kept the conversation going, asking her about ten times about her recent injury and if she were okay enough to walk. Meg nodded after every query, loping along and trying to keep pace, occasionally piping in with monosyllabic answers to his questions. When she came to a stop, across the street from her house, she pointed to it and managed to let him know that it was indeed where she lived, all without uttering a word.

"Oh I was pretty sure that was your place. You had better put some ice on that shin, Meg. It will bruise for sure. I will see you tomorrow!" As he started up the hill and through the woods, he called back over his shoulder, "Oh, there is another practice game next week!"

All she could manage was a wave and a shaky smile.

Meg limped through the red door and muttered something unintelligible to her mother, something about not being hungry. Then heading directly to her room she slammed the door shut, wondering why her heart was thumping so loudly in her chest.

CHAPTER 19

MARY

Mary met Meg on Main Street, and they headed out for their second day of school. Yesterday morning, after skidding into the building with seconds to spare, they had decided to meet even earlier that next morning, to time it properly. Precision was important to Meg, as Mary knew only too well. As soon as the two girls set out on their way, Meg checked her watch, nodded and then burst out in one very long paragraph.

"Mary. Remember I told you that I hoped I would see Vic? Or run into him once school started? He was always so nice to Sarah and me when we were at their home, but I never thought much of it, as he was older and in high school and I figured he was just being nice because we were there with his mom. Well now that I am, actually now that we are both in high school, we are with him. Well he is two years older so obviously not exactly with him. Anyway I did run into him. Actually I bumped into him, in the halls, literally, yesterday. More than bumped. In all seriousness, I crashed right into him. Once I could stammer away about where I was headed, he helped me find my class as you and I know how much I stress over that, you know, my panic of being lost in school and late for classes. Later, after the collision sequence, we kind of hung out a bit. And I was looking for you all day. You and I have zero classes together by the way and I am so bummed. Anyway, I couldn't wait to talk to you. I was going to call you last night but I was afraid all the big ears in the house would be listening. I knew we could talk today and I rationalized that that would be soon enough. So there is more. I went to his soccer game yesterday, after band. Sorry I forgot to tell you about that. Well I never even saw you so I couldn't have told you as it turns out. I hope you didn't wait for me. Again, sorry. Back to the game part of my day. So, he plays Varsity and he is really, really good and his mom was supposed to come but she never did. Then, you know what a klutz I am, I walloped my leg against the side of the bleacher, and just look at this lump on my shin, but it is better now and he was really worried about it and told me to put ice on it later and he was right because it really did help and anyway he kind of walked me home or maybe he walked and I hobbled the same way and I thought maybe I was having a heart attack when I went through the front door and I went right to bed last night without dinner and what on earth is wrong with me?"

"Well, first of all, breathe. At least once." Mary and Meg had been best friends for as long as they could remember and there was nothing that they did not know about each other. Mary patiently waited for Meg to finish catching her breath and continue. First, because it took Mary a minute or so to absorb all of what the girl had said so rapidly. Second, she figured that there might be a chance that even more might be added after Meg finally took that recommended breath. There almost always was more.

As predicted, there was indeed a coda. "And then he said that his mom asked him to check up on me and that she missed me and oh my goodness I think I have a crush on him but well actually I did have a sort of little crush on him in middle school but this is different and so much more than that."

Mary smiled. She knew her best friend well. That didn't take long this time. Meg usually managed to figure things out after a speech, or a diatribe. Usually it took a day or two. Never before had Meg's final analysis been this instantaneous. "Exactly, my friend. You are seriously crushing. You got it bad."

"But Mary, he is so gorgeous. He is even better looking now than he was in middle school. Remember how cute we thought he was back then? But he is a junior. A Junior! And I think, no I am certain, that all the girls like him. All those cheerleader types. I don't stand a chance. He is completely out of my league."

"Meg." Mary tried to be the voice of reason. "Have you ever actually looked at you? I mean, you have mirrors in that house of yours, do you not? You are definitely not too shabby." Mary grabbed her arm. "Seriously, you are beautiful. Everyone but you knows that."

"I don't know Mary, you are so kind to me. And you probably need glasses."

"I will have to check this out. Not my eyes, as I see perfectly. I mean I will have to check out this new and improved and older Vic Becker. I do like his name, by the way. It sort of sounds like he should be in the movies."

Meg stopped in her tracks, a goofy smile pinned on her face.

"Come on, lovebird. Snap out of it! We will be late!" Mary fitted her hand into the crook of Meg's arm, dragging her forward as they headed off to school.

CHAPTER 20

MEG

Whether it was just happenstance, conflicting class schedules or if he were indeed avoiding her (which was her most obsessive fear) Meg did not see Victor again until the soccer game that next week. She had dragged Mary with her as it was a day off from dance class so both of their afternoons were free. Plus, Meg was able to tell her mom when she left in the morning that she was spending the afternoon with Mary and she wouldn't be lying. Just avoiding actual facts. Her moral self was okay with that.

The two best friends sat side by side, waiting for the game to begin.

"I don't know, Mary. Maybe we shouldn't have come. Maybe he avoided me this week because he thinks I am an idiot. Maybe I am making too much of this. Maybe he....but wait, he did tell me last week that I should come, so I guess it is fine that we are here. But maybe he wasn't asking me, exactly. Maybe he was just stating a fact? No. I think he did mean it as an invitation." Mary just smiled at her. No need to respond at all to all the "maybes" since Meg had already self-answered, right in the middle of her own questions.

Just before the second half, Meg felt a gentle tap on her shoulder and a lightly accented voice whispered, "Meg!" Meg turned back and looked up at the familiar face that belonged to the voice she knew so well, azure eyes hidden by sunglasses, and white-blond hair tucked up into a baseball cap, mostly out of view except for a few unruly wisps peaking out from the sides.

Both friends said hello, and Elke responded. "Hello Mary, good to see you again! And Meg, I am so glad that you came! I am so sorry I missed you last week. Victor told me he hoped we could both catch up today!"

"How is everything?" Meg, asked, over her left shoulder while still keeping one eye on the game. "And how are the horses?"

"All is fine and they are good, Meg. And how do you girls like high school?"

"It's great!" Meg and Mary answered, almost simultaneously.

"Meg. Can I just talk with you, for a moment. Back there, behind the bleachers. Mary, do you mind if we step away for a bit?"

"Of course not! Besides, I have to try to figure out this game!" Mary turned back to concentrate on the players in the field.

Meg and Elke stepped out over the metal bleacher seats and walked around to the back of the seating area. Elke began, carefully. "Meg, I know Mary probably knows everything, as she is your best friend, but I just needed to talk to you alone for a moment. Even though it all happened almost a year ago, so much has been bothering me about things with your mom. I feel dreadful, and I know that it hasn't been easy for you and Sarah. But there is something else that has been troubling me so much and I wanted to find just the right opportunity to talk with you. Way back, on that horrible day when Sarah fell, I heard things. Even though I might have missed most of it, what I heard was not good. I was certain that the words that were spoken were done so out of anger and frustration, but still, they were said. Once words are released, they are impossible to retract. Anyway, all I can tell you is this one thing, and I guess it is more like advice. Meg. You must never carry the weight of guilt on your shoulders. There is a reason they call occurrences, like what happened to Sarah, accidents."

"Ooh, you heard that part. Yeah. I know. But Mrs. Becker, she wasn't wrong. It was my fault. I wasn't watching. I should have been paying more attention. She is my little sister and I was in charge."

"Meg. How old were you? Twelve? You were just a little girl yourself."

"Yes, I know. But sometimes I think that in the end it is just easier for her to blame me. It takes the load off of her own guilt. Because down deep I feel like she does believe that she is at fault. She should have been there. For both of us."

"Perhaps. But it is a burden you should not have to carry. It will eat away at you, Meg. Please don't let that happen." Elke gave her a hug. "Now, let's go watch this game!"

"Yes! And thank you, Mrs. Becker." And they headed back to the bleachers. They bantered on, all through the second half, and filled each other in on all of their adventures. As the game ended, Victor headed over to the bleachers.

"Ah, my two favorite girls!" He said as he hugged his mother, brushing by Meg's now stunned and currently mute self.

"Flattery, as always, will get you everywhere! Great game, Victor." Elke kissed him on the cheek.

"Thanks. Hi Meg! And you must be Mary?" He took Mary's hand and shook it firmly. "My mother has told me many stories about you. I heard you are the star ballerina."

Meg caught the look on Mary's face, and she knew precisely what had just happened to her best friend. Currently under the very same spell, they were both in a trance and speechless. How did he keep doing that?

And what was that he just said? His two favorite girls?

"Meg. Mary. Can I give you a ride home?" Elke, as always, knew the correct time to intervene and change course.

The two teenagers looked at each other and then back at the two Beckers and nodded.

Mary was the one to first gain control of her manners followed by control of her vocal cords and said, "Yes, please. Thank you!"

Victor sat up front and the girls climbed into the back seat of the Buick.

"Great car, Mrs. Becker!" Mary said as they headed home. Meg was still mute.

"It is an older car, but it was born the same year as Victor, 1956. I think he might be a bit embarrassed about it, but he will still use it when he gets his license later this year. Even if it is old fashioned! Listen, I think I should drop you both somewhere other than home for you, Meg. Not so sure the Pedersen household will like me pulling into the driveway. Maybe at Mary's house? If that is okay."

"No problem. Good idea! I live on Park Place. Next street over." Mary pointed it out.

The girls slid out of the back seat, and Mary thanked the Beckers and Meg managed a smile and a wave.

Mary turned to Meg, once the Beckers had pulled out of the driveway. "Oh boy, Meg. Now I know why you have completely lost all of your senses. You are in trouble. BIG trouble. And not, for once, with your mom."

CHAPTER 21

VIC

Elke said basically the same words to Victor as they left Meg and Mary and headed home.

It happened faster than they anticipated. Vic, whether subconsciously or otherwise found himself standing near Meg's classroom door immediately after each period ended. He couldn't help himself. Memorizing her schedule early on, he would make it look as though he were coincidentally in the same place as she was, at any given time. Not quite comprehending this new magnetic pull, he found himself helpless in its power.

Ritual became habit, and he found himself walking her home on the days that they were both free after school. Always careful to keep out of sight, Victor would separate from her early, veering across the street well in advance, to head to the woods, just in case watchful eyes were on them. She went to every soccer game, and Mrs. Becker would bring her back, leaving her safely each time at Mary's house.

Without actually stating as much, they were heading into the boyfriend/girlfriend zone. Taking it slowly at first, they were apprehensive about the possibility of ruining what had started out as a good friendship. They both knew more was coming, soon, even though Meg's mom would surely object. Especially if and when she found out who Vic was. So they were incredibly cautious.

It got easier, the talking part, with time. Since Meg began to share, more and more, Victor did so as well. They ran everything by each other. Meg explained how difficult the year had been when Sarah was hit by the car. She expressed her guilt, still, even all these years later. It had been horrifying. She also explained that her parents had been about to break up beforehand, and how the accident brought her parents unintentional clarity and a turnaround. She said things were just a little better after the accident. Within a year, though, things had reverted back to their own dysfunctional normal. Eventually Meg shared with Vic her fears about how much alcohol was a problem in their home.

Victor shared with Meg how odd he felt he was, living where he did. He didn't discuss his mother's other life, the healing part, though. He was half-embarrassed, half-proud of his mother. But he loved her, and loved all the animals as well. Although sometimes he felt like he lived in a zoo. He never mentioned his father. He was relieved that Meg never asked. Not directly, at least. She did hint, though.

"So, you know my Dad was born in Denmark?And my mom was born in Canada. Her parents immigrated from Scotland. They met after my dad immigrated to Canada, to Hamilton, for a job. My mom worked there as well, in the same stainless steel factory. That was back in the fifties. Then they moved here, to

Beauville, right before I was born. And so, I have always lived here. Your mom said you were born in Germany?"

She had ended her statement as a question, but he decided he wouldn't elaborate on that point. Vic finished off the last of his cone, and started to get up. Time to change the subject. "Yes, I was born there. Hey, we should head back now."

Victor knew that she wanted more information, but his was a story that would be difficult to tell. It had been hard for him as well to hear it, when his mom finally explained the hows and whys of her tale. Now wasn't the time. He grabbed her hand and they headed out of the ice cream shop, and walked smack dab into Mrs. Pedersen.

"Mom, hi!" Meg sputtered. Then, gathering herself said, "Mom, this is my friend, Vic." Mrs. Pedersen, surprised, stopped in her tracks. "Oh. Hello."

Victor, who had immediately let go of Meg's hand the second he saw the woman, stuck out his right hand, and attempted to shake Mrs. Pedersen's hand. "Pleased to meet you, Ma'am."

Ignoring him, she turned to Meg. "When will you be home?" "Soon, mom."

And then she was gone.

CHAPTER 22

EVELYN

By never quite acknowledging that her daughter had a boy in her life, Evelyn Pedersen took the route of denial. Basically ignoring Vic on the occasions when he had gathered enough nerve to stop by the house, she chose to feign blindness. By not being able to "see" it, it wasn't actually happening. Her other alternative was worse. If she were to let on that she knew everything, and subsequently made the effort to thwart this new and obviously blossoming relationship, it would most likely boomerang. Inevitably, the relationship would become more serious, out of defiance. Meg was like that, combative and rebellious.

Evelyn had indeed found out, early on, that this boy was Victor Becker. His resemblance to his mother was uncanny. Incapable of being able to stop herself, or comprehend why she actually detested Victor's mother, she let the darkness of hatred envelop her. Deeper than her initial anger towards the woman, this new feeling began welling in her gut. Any person possessing a semblance of self-confidence might simply look at Elke as a kind person who had come into their daughters' lives. But deep inside Evelyn dwelt a psyche possessing a zero measure of self-worth. Perceiving this other woman as a threat, for no accountable reason, Evelyn took on this hatred as a simpler method of justifying her rationale.

However an issue burrowed much more profoundly than that. For Evelyn what was most vexing and perplexing was how Elke had managed to have a such a wonderful relationship with Meg and Sarah. All of this had occurred in a relatively short period of time, something she had never been able to achieve herself with her own daughters. For years and years.

Simply defined, what Evelyn was actually feeling was pure envy.

CHAPTER 23

VIC

Meg and Vic were officially dating by her fifteenth birthday in late October. He took her out for dinner, and kissed her goodnight for the first time. It was turning into an easy, comfortable and happy relationship. Saturday was date night, and they would often take the train from the station in the middle of town, and head into New York City. Sometimes they would find discount theater tickets, or just wander about, exploring the city that was so very different from their own suburban town.

One night, on a nighttime train ride home, Vic finally opened up to Meg and shared a story that wasn't easy to tell.

"Meg, I'm sorry I have been so distant about this. I know you have asked, about my father and about my past." He took her hand as he began to explain all that he and his mother had gone through. The seats around them were empty and the only surrounding sound was the train moving rhythmically over the tracks.

"We're studying World War II in history class this year. I'm in the middle now of writing a paper, and while in the library doing research, a lot of the stuff my mom told me about is in the encyclopedias that I was looking through. I figured it was time, as I know you are curious about it. I need to let you in on the story. I mean what my mom and I went through, well really just my mom as I was too little to know what was up."

He went on. "My mom never kept secrets from me, and when I got old enough to ask, I had probably too many annoying questions. But she answered all of them. Now that you and I know each other so well, and since you are friends with my mom, and also I kinda need to tell someone, I figured I could trust you with our story." He stopped for a second, took a sip of the cola he had brought on the train, and then continued.

"Okay. Here goes. My mom was born in 1934, in East Berlin, before things got really messy with the onset of the war. Her parents were Jewish, and they, as you can rightly guess, lived in fear as the years went on that they would be taken away. They wouldn't have known where they were going at that time. But we all know now that it would have been to concentration camps. My mother, unusually blond and blue eyed, actually looked more German, more Aryan than most of their Jewish friends, and so, her parents started to concoct a scheme. She was their only child. They had to save her." Victor turned to look directly into Meg's eyes.

"So this is the time in history where I am with my paper, so I have the dates in my head pretty clear. War broke out on September 1, 1939, and the government started restrictions on the German Jews. They had a mandatory curfew and the Jewish people were not allowed to enter certain areas. They also got less rations than non-Jews. On top of that, they had to hand over valuables and things like bicycles and radios to help the war effort. Well, that was what they were told. In September of 1941, all Jews over the age of six had to wear the Jewish Star on their outer garments, visible to all. That was the moment when my mom's parents needed to move forward with their scheme. It was what they had to do, because my mother was seven."

Meg, riveted, held onto Vic's hand more tightly.

"Their neighbors, the Beckers, had been their friends for years. My mom used to play with the Becker children every day, and she blended into their large family, almost like another sibling. The Beckers often joked that she was their sixth child. On that day, when they were handing out the stars, my mom's parents knew that needed to act really quickly."

Vic stopped a second, and then went on.

"Okay, I'm not a textbook, so I hope that the details all fall into place. Anyway, my grandparents went to see the Beckers with their idea and thankfully, the kind family was happy to help. Mr. Becker worked for the government, and he knew how to get around the system. Falsifying paperwork, he managed to create a birth document that said that my mother was one of their children. She moved into their home. They had to do some finagling with the school, but the headmaster was friends with Mr. Becker, and everyone kept the secret."

Victor paused again, and then went on with the tale. Meg put her head on his shoulder, and just listened.

"Not long after that, my mother's parents disappeared. They were all never sure if they ended up in Auschwitz, or if they had figured out a way to escape. My mother never saw them again, though. They never heard a word, and so they assumed the worst." Tears started to stream down Meg's cheeks. She wiped at them with her sleeve. Victor went on.

"The years passed, and the war ended, but things were not wonderful in East Berlin. Throughout those years, my mom's memories of her own parents faded. Although she still has one really aged photo of the two of them, it is hard for her today to envision them. The picture is upstairs in her room, next to her bed. I will show it to you if you get the chance to come over." He went on.

"She attended school, as Elke Becker and then eventually went on to nursing school. Then here comes the tricky part. When she was eighteen, what had started out as a really close friendship with the eldest Becker, Werner, turned into a lot more than that. They had fallen in love." Victor smiled at that point and handed her the napkin he had received with his soda. Meg dabbed at her wet cheeks.

"This was not an easy love story. First of all, in the eyes of the authorities, with the forged documents, they were technically brother and sister. So, a few years later, when they decided to marry, it needed to be done in secret with a friend as the officiant and the Becker family members were the only people in attendance. She was already Elke Becker. No need to change her name. That was in 1955. My mom was twenty-one. She found out she was pregnant a few months later. And that is when things got really complicated."

Meg unusually silent, sat there, transfixed, listening to a story that seemed impossible, yet was completely true.

"My mother gave birth to me, in the house. On December 30th, 1956. And they managed to keep it hidden. It was a big house. But, when I turned two, they knew it was time. Time to do something. They couldn't hide a little boy forever, and I was growing and getting into mischief." He smiled a little crookedly at that. Meg smiled back. A needed break. If only for a moment.

"My parents decided they would need to leave East Berlin for sure, and Germany as well. So, with some pretty much illegal connections, Werner's father put together forged travel documents. They had to get a birth document for me too."

Vic stopped for a moment. "We, my mom and I, managed to get out of East Berlin, but because of the political issues there at the time, we could never return. Our documents were a made up medical excuse to go only to London, and then return. But we never did, of course. London was our first stop. Then we headed on to New York City, where a Becker cousin would sponsor us until my dad could get away."

Vic took a little respite, giving Meg a hug. For her, but mostly for himself. It was always hard thinking about the father he only knew when he was just a baby, a father he wished he could know now. "My father worked for the government, like my grandfather, and it wasn't easy for him to just up and leave. Mostly because he was opposed to life in East Berlin, and was vocal about it. They were keeping an eye on him."

Meg looked up into his eyes. "Your mom said that you are fluent in German, and that she spoke to you in both languages. But only in English when others are around. And that she tries to hide her accent, even today."

"Correct. And she has always kept a low profile. Habit, I guess. Sorry. This is a long story. But I really want you to know it…Anyway, we had moved to the states, and my mom needed work. Since she didn't have her nurse training certificates here, and she couldn't prove it, she had to take a lesser position in a hospital, as an aide. She had found a job, with the help of the cousin in New York City who had a contact in White Plains, where she still works now. But we couldn't afford to live down there, so we headed north, up to Beauville where she found an abandoned cottage. In the late 50's land where we live now was really reasonable, as it had originally been all summer homes near the lake. I think it must have been the same for your parents. They came from another country, too, right?Around the same time?"

"Yes, I think so. I was born here, in New York, in 1958, so yes. Probably. Funny they never met!"

Vic went on. "Yeah. True. Anyway, my mother made a down payment on the cottage, but it needed a lot of work. My father had given her all the money he could collect, before she and I left. The money was running low, but, by saving as much as she could and living simply, we were able to survive. She has a green thumb and got the gardens and green house to grow us a lot of our food."

Victor continued. "My mom started taking in animals, like the chickens and horses, when people could no longer take care of them. Or they would just appear, sometimes in the middle of the night. She has a way with them, and helps with their injuries." He kept this part vague, as he didn't really want Meg to know, just yet, exactly what his mother did. Although he suspected that she actually did know much more than she let on.

"I know, Vic. She healed my cat. And Sarah as well." Meg smiled up at him. "Vic, that is an incredible story. But wait, what happened with your father?"

"We got a few letters from him, through his cousin in New York. But then they stopped. By 1961, when the Berlin Wall was put up, it made communication nearly impossible. We did hear a few things, second hand. One story told us that he had tried to escape, and that he had been shot and put in hospital. Another was that they had imprisoned him. He was a rebel, and they had been watching his moves. Not sure exactly what he did, but it was enough for him to be taken away. Anyway, contact has been difficult. My mom has sent letters, but most are returned, unopened."

The train pulled into the station in Beauville and they disembarked, walking arm and arm to Meg's house.

"Meg, I don't know where my father is now. Or even if he is alive. But I have my mom, and she is both parents to me."

"Your mom is an amazing person, Vic. Thank you so much for letting me know this about her. And you."

"There is even more. I never really noticed it when I was little, but she made certain, always, that I was fed before she would eat. Often we had only a little bit of food. She would say she wasn't hungry and would then give me seconds. She said she never ate much during the war, and that was why she is so petite and didn't need to eat as much as her growing son. She always, always put me first. She is the most selfless person I have ever known."

Victor kissed her goodnight and headed back up the path through the woods towards his home.

CHAPTER 24

CARL

"Dad," Meg had stopped by Carl's study early one evening after dinner. "Do you have a minute?"

"For you dear, always. Or I might even have an hour if you need it!" He had been pouring over a stack of papers, his glasses perched near the tip of his nose. His once red hair was now a silvery gray, close cropped. Looking up at his daughter, he waited for what he assumed would be a question for school, some project she was working on. He was intrigued. "Go on!"

"Thanks, Dad. Listen. I know you were in the Resistance, in Denmark, during the War. World War II. I was hoping maybe you could help me with something. I need to do some research."

He saw that she was hesitating, and wondered if there weren't more to this question, more depth to provide direction where she was going. "Of course, Meg. But why this sudden interest? School assignment?"

"Well, no, not exactly. Okay, so not at all school. More personal. Look, Dad, I know that you are all not that thrilled with Vic. Or rather that Mom is not that thrilled with Vic, but there is so much more to their story, Vic and his Mom's story, more that actually might make Mom warm her heart a bit."

As best as she could detail, she told her dad the story Victor had told her that night on the train. When she finished, Carl stood up without a word and went to the bookshelf behind his desk. He pulled out a small brown leather book, and opened it up. All written in Danish, he scanned through until he found the set of numbers carefully written next to a man's name, a man he hadn't seen or heard from in years.

"Meg. It is after midnight in Europe right now. I will wait til the morning, and I will see what I can do." Hudson had jumped up on the desk, and Carl gave the cat a scratch behind his right ear. Noticing that his daughter was still lingering, he queried, "Meg, is there something else on your mind?"

Sitting herself down in the chair facing his desk, she breathed what appeared to be a sigh of relief before answering. "Yes. I think so. Though not sure how to say it exactly."

"Well, give it a go!"

"Okay, so Dad, did you ever feel so comfortable with a person that you felt as though you had always known them?"

Carefully pondering a bit, he then answered his daughter. "Well, yes. I have. It does happen, when people connect immediately, that there is a feeling of familiarity going beyond just that moment in time. There are reasons for that. Common interests, similar backgrounds and relatable upbringing can make an initial meeting turn rapidly into a friendship, or even more. Your mother's aunt Janet used to talk about kindred spirits, people sharing a mutual connection that is meaningful. Also, some feel that there is actual love at first sight. I guess that all of this does and can happen."

Still scratching the now loudly purring cat, Carl added, "I am assuming this is what you are feeling with your young man?"

Meg nodded.

Carl continued. "However, there are some people that believe that this instant familiarity you are talking about can come from something completely different. This is, in fact, a bit of a stretch to some. Although I was hesitant at first to acknowledge it, it all made complete sense to me as the years move forward. As you know, I did spend quite a bit of time in India, back in my twenties. We had a problem, for a while, in the factory where I was working, with a major ant infestation. You are probably wondering where I am going with this! Well, it turned out that the night watchman had the full belief that all life was sacred, that all souls reincarnated and he was convinced that some of his family members might just have returned as ants. So he was leaving out food for them!"

Meg laughed at that, but then asked. "Interesting. But what exactly is reincarnation?"

"I asked the same question, all those years ago! The answer I got made sense. Perhaps. Some feel that reincarnation is a philosophical concept, others agree that it is more of a religious concept. Basically, it is the theory that after biological death the non-physical essence of a living being begins a new existence in a different body. Some call it rebirth, some call in transmigration. Many believe that the souls of humans can only go into another human, not into an animal or even an insect like that watchman believed. Animals do have souls, though." He pulled Hudson onto his shoulder and gave him a hug. "That is for certain. Not so certain about insects, though! Part of me would feel dreadful after squashing a fly, if there were indeed a soul there!"

Carl could see Meg's mind computing, not quite listening. "Okay. I see, but how is this related to the familiarity thing?"

"Sorry. I got off track a bit. I did do some exploring into this, as you know I had faced a bit of a near death situation while there. I was extremely sick, after contracting Malaria and then Hepatitis. I guess I was feeling a bit mortal at the time, and I was looking for the hopeful possibility of some kind of life after death. I had an East Indian doctor treating me, and he gave me some solace in that department. With all of his medical knowledge I was intrigued that he also believed in something that wasn't at all scientific. He assured me that souls do indeed return, and that often they return to family circles. That soul of the grandmother might just return as her newborn grandchild. Going into even more depth with me, he also talked about instant connections, which was why I was reminded of all of this when you asked me. According to him, an unusual connection to a stranger, or when looking into another's eyes and getting the feeling that you already know them, means that your souls have been together. Before. In another life. Maybe you and the Beckers were friends at another point in time?" Carl winked at his daughter.

"Hmmm. Interesting thought, Dad. That might explain it. Because I feel incredibly close to them, in such a short amount of time. But I also feel really close with Mary, and I have known her all my life." She went over and hugged him and kissed him on the cheek. Then, giving Hudson a pet, said "Hey Dad, maybe you were a cat once. You do seem to have nine lives!"

CHAPTER 25

MEG

That next day, while in study hall, which was thankfully held in the library, Meg went to the reference section, and pulled out every book she could find about post World War II in Germany. Pouring over the encyclopedia, and a few history books, she began jotting down everything she could find. She wanted to understand, and needed to understand. She compiled her notes so that she could be ready for the next step.

She began to assemble the facts of the where and when of the Berlin Wall. With careful attention to detail, she read through the information, in her head, once her research was compiled.

During the last days of World War II, in February 1945, the Allies' Yalta Conference had divided Germany into four occupation zones. Great Britain, France and the United States were to occupy the western and southern portions. The Soviet Union was to occupy the eastern side. Located in Soviet territory, the city of Berlin was also divided into its own zones.

In 1949, the western and southern zones occupied by Britain, France and the United States become West Germany. This was known as The Federal Republic of Germany. East Germany, located in the Soviet zone became The German Democratic Republic. West Germany became a democratic republic. East Germany became a Communist country, and was aligned with the Soviet Union.

During the years 1949 to 1961, over two million East Germans escaped to the West. At that time, East Berliners needed a special pass to be able to leave. However, foreign citizens, West Germans, West Berliners and Allied military personnel were allowed to enter East Berlin.

On August 13, 1961, the Communist government of East Germany built a wall separating East and West Berlin. The wall evolved into a concrete barrier that was heavily fortified. There were guards, traps and other obstacles to impede flight. Between East and West Berlin the wall stood eleven to thirteen feet high. It stretched 28 miles. The Wall also encircled the city of West Berlin, stretching about one hundred miles. Behind the barriers, buildings were razed and the remaining area was known as 'no man's land' or the 'death strip.' Guards in more than three hundred sentry towers would and could shoot anyone trying to escape.

Meg stopped writing for a moment, making connections to the facts. Based on what Vic had told her, they had escaped before the actual wall was constructed. Vic had said they had documents, and that must have been this pass that was mentioned. Only they never came back. Thankfully they knew that things were about to worsen. This wall was clearly meant to deter any and all escape. Mines and wires were underneath it. Pipes on top prevented scaling. Many died from falls during their escape attempts or by being shot by guards. It must have been terrifying. She continued writing down the information. Other countries had tried to help, including the United States, by stationing troops in West Germany. President Kennedy gave a speech in West Berlin, encouraging freedom in June of 1963.

Then, in September of 1971 an agreement was made which allowed for West Berlin and East Berlin to import and export goods. At that point, the reference material ended. It was currently 1973. Surely there was more to the story. Meg went to the newspaper section, pouring through the information more recent than the publication of the encyclopedia. And all she could find was that there had been a treaty in December of 1972 signed by both West and East Germany that normalized diplomatic relations, and recognized each other's sovereignty.

"Good. Maybe things are better now. Maybe just a little." She said the words out loud to herself as she jotted down the last of the information, just in time, as the period bell was ringing.

That night she shared what she had learned with her father. She was hopeful, she told him. Things are getting better over there. Maybe they had a chance. A slim chance, at best, to help.

CHAPTER 26

CARL

"Aksel, good morning. Ah yes, I received your packet and it looks like this might indeed be possible. I won't tell her anything yet, as I don't want to get her hopes up. You and I know that these things can go south rapidly. This is a tricky one, that is for certain. I thank you for your assistance in the matter. I will hopefully be able to return the favor some day."

Carl was quiet as his friend spoke. His Danish was a bit rusty as he was out of practice, so it took him a bit longer to respond. He had been working so hard to perfect his English that his Danish speaking skills were often neglected. He hoped his wording wasn't stilted and that he conveyed his intentions properly. Aksel was an old and admired friend.

"No, Aksel, you do not owe me a thing. By the way I am looking forward to reading your book. Happy to hear that you put the atrocities, all those horrific things, into words for others to better understand. This is a very important thing that you have done. " He paused, listening to his friend. "You flatter me, but no, I am doing nothing here that is even remotely incredible. It may not even work, but I must at least make an effort. This means so much to my daughter. You have daughters, no? You would move the mountains for them as well."

He hung up the phone and arranged the clippings and papers, checking and rechecking the information that they contained.

CHAPTER 27

MEG

Meg kept her research and her request for her father's help quiet, not wanting to tell Vic just yet. She had a plan gelling in her head, an idea that she might be able help him, and Elke, too, of course. She knew her father was doing what he could as well. Her dad told her he was waiting for his friend to get more information. And so, they would be patient. She hoped that she could give this information as a gift for Christmas. Or actually for Hanukah, as both Vic and his mother were Jewish and did not celebrate Christian holidays.

Thanksgiving was coming, and Meg thought it would be nice to have Vic come for dinner at their home. He and his mom did not really celebrate the holiday, as it wasn't a German thing. Well, it wasn't a Danish or Canadian thing either except Canadians did their own version, the second Monday in October. So her family did an adaptation of the event, on the appointed American day in November.

She broached the subject with her father first, as she knew he would soften the idea once he conveyed it to his wife. She did, of course, bristle at the thought but reluctantly agreed. As long as he didn't bring his mother.

It was a rather uncomfortable evening, at first, but in the end Meg was glad that he had come. Her dad had really enjoyed talking to him, as Vic was smart and funny and interesting. Vic also bent over backwards flattering her mom, complementing her cooking, and then thanked her profusely when he left. When the door closed behind him her mother actually smiled.

"Well, he is most certainly a fine young man." Which she immediately ruined with "Despite the fact that he is German and a Jew and was born to that intolerable woman."

CHAPTER 28

Vic

"Come on, let's go!" Vic grabbed Meg by the hand and headed her up to the path through the woods. "No one will see, and besides, you haven't been to my place in over a year."

"Ooooh, boy. Not sure, Vic. But I guess it will be ok."

It was one of those remarkably warm early December afternoons, with the last gasps of fall still lingering in the air. They had gone for a walk into town, when Vic suddenly remembered he had promised to help his mom with a project in the barn. Reluctant to leave Meg so early in their day together, he figured they should just take the chance and go for it. Besides, it was time. "Mom will be thrilled and even better, maybe you can help."

They headed up the familiar meandering path, tromping over the deciduous debris. Since most leaves had already fallen and begun their decay, the only trees blocking the sunlight were the enormous pines. The clearing began coming into view early on.

Vic was so absorbed in looking forward, and chatting away with Meg who was following closely behind him that it took a moment to realize she hadn't said anything for a bit. Noticing that not only was she being silent, he looked back and discovered that she wasn't even there. At least not there in his line of vision. Calling out for her and not hearing a response compelled him to start to run back down the hilly path.

Finally finding her, lying near a birch tree, he raced to her side. Instinct took over and he reached for her wrist and checked her pulse.

"Meg. Meg. Are you okay?"

No response. Without thinking he started tracing his hands over her head, as it appeared as though she had struck it somehow. Resting his hands near her forehead, he almost jumped out of his skin when he realized that there was a soft light, a violet light, emanating from just above her brow. Wait, he had it too?

Panic made him do what he could never have imagined himself doing. As he had observed, many times, he looked up to the sky, as his mother did. She never thought he was actually paying attention, but he was glad now that he had been watching her. Completely out of curiosity. Not sure which words his mother actually said to whatever source she spoke to, he decided to just utter what was in his heart. He called out to the universe, begging whomever might be listening, begging for her to be okay.

"Vic?"

"Meg! You are okay! You scared me." Pulling her gently up into a hug he said softly, almost in a whisper but mainly to himself, "Actually you scared me a ton, but I think I also just scared myself to death."

Helping her to her feet, he guided her the rest of the way. "I want my mom to look at you." Hesitating a second, he added, "Just in case I messed up or something."

Elke was there, at the clearing, waiting for them. She gave her son a penetrating look, one that needed no words, communicating to Vic that she was fully aware of what had just transpired. How, he wasn't exactly sure. But today had been a day of firsts, so there was no rationale possible. He would just continue to go with the inevitable flow.

Elke pulled Meg into a hug, one that Vic was certain was meant more for an assessment than for a greeting. She pulled away and with her eyes, examined the girl thoroughly, head to toe. Focusing back again on the girl's eyes, Elke said, quietly, "Meg, my dear girl. I think you are fine, now. But still, come on inside and sit down and I will make some herbal tea." With another knowing look, she stared straight into her son's eyes once more. "For both of you."

The two teenagers sat at the kitchen table, both with baffled looks on their faces. Meg sipped at her tea, not talking. Victor did the same, thinking how very awkward this day had become "Meg," Elke started. "I need to hear how things felt for you, before and after the fall. Especially just before you woke up."

Meg started to explain. "It was really, really weird. I think I wasn't really paying attention to the path. Pretty sure I tripped over a root. But I don't remember anything after that. I was just lying there, and I couldn't move. Like I was asleep. In complete darkness. After a bit, I heard words, coming from somewhere, although they sounded like they were coming from underwater and reverberating around me. Kind of like an echo. But I wasn't aware of their source. It sounded like the way a voice comes to you in a dream. Everything around me was as black as night. But then, all at once I saw a tiny pinpoint of a pale purple light forming in front of my eyes. The light grew and expanded and with it came a warm and soft feeling, a feeling that surrounded me like a blanket. Or a hug. When I opened my eyes I could see a hand. Vic's hand. His fingertips were laying across my forehead, and his palm was resting across the tip of my nose. He was pressing down gently and looking at me with his big blue eyes."

"Good. Very good." Elke looked contemplative, satisfied, yet still a bit hesitant.

"Mrs. Becker, how does it happen. This healing thing that you do."And then Meg looked quickly at Vic, "That I think, perhaps, Vic just did?"

"I wish I knew why. Or how. I have learned to accept that it just IS. There is nothing I can do to stop it. It comes from within, somewhere. I have always had it, I guess. I just didn't realize I had it until I was a teenager. What happened to me back then was sort of what I think just happened to Vic." She looked at her son and took his hand in hers. "The most important thing that I can say is that it comes from goodness, and from a place of love. And it comes from an inner need to help."

CHAPTER 29

CARL

"Meg, I think I have something." Carl Pedersen led his daughter into his office. "I finally got some concrete information on Werner Becker. Come look."

Carl, a bit more confident now, felt it was time to let his daughter know that there had been some progress. He brought out a folder, a folder he had simply labeled WB, and opened it up to reveal several sheets of paper. On top was a tattered clipping from a newspaper with a blurry image of a group of men. Underneath was a caption, in what Meg assumed was German. But the words were fuzzy, as if it had gotten wet and the ink had bled.

"Meg, my German is a bit foggy now, but I still remember most of what I learned in school. This photo appears to be a government group, an office photo. And the article below is discussing how a few of them from this office had been arrested. This newspaper was from 1962."

"So a year after the wall was erected?" Meg chimed in.

"Yes. I see that you have done your homework," Carl smiled proudly at his daughter. "And I am sure you have discovered just how oppressive life was then and still is today, in 1973, in East Berlin."

"It doesn't seem real. That people would construct a wall like that."

"Exactly, Meg. Some say that the wall was built to keep the country's people in. However, the East German and Soviet Governments said it was for keeping Capitalism out. They knew that people were fleeing the East, once the lines were drawn. When the numbers became enormous, they knew that they needed to keep what they could. What transpired actually ended up alienating them. It was lucky Vic and his mom did what they did. She sounds like a very impressive woman."

Meg nodded at his remark. "Yes, Dad, she is incredible."

Busily studying the clipping and staring at the caption under the photo again she said excitedly. "Wait, it is hard to make out, but does this say Herr Becker?"

"Yes. It does. I assume that this is Victor's father. And from what I can make out from this article, it seems that he and a few of his fellow workers were involved in some, shall we say, rebellious acts against the government. Not a good thing as technically they were government workers themselves. Clearly it was an internal rebellion."

"Exactly what Vic had said. I mean he figured out what must have happened. He said his dad had tried to escape, to come to the United States. That had been the plan. But he said that there were complications. His father, Werner, was a known rebel. It is also possible that he was shot. While escaping, and that the authorities were looking for them."

Carl looked down at his hands a moment, deep in thought. It took a minute to look up, as he was in the midst of internally drawing the parallels, and the similarities with his own life. In the Resistance. He himself had been shot, rebelling Nazi forces in Denmark. Clearly, it seemed like Vic's father had been doing the same. Only this time it was a German rebelling the Soviets. "Meg, I will piece all of this together. It might take some time."

"Dad, whatever you do will be more than they have been able to. Thank you so very much. I knew you would do this. I knew you would help." She kissed him on the cheek.

CHAPTER 30

Vic

"Meg, we have to talk." Vic grabbed her hand as they walked out of the school building, heading into town. Soccer season had ended, and so they had much more time together as the late autumn days began to take on the normal chill. A few soft wet flakes started falling, and they tucked into the little gazebo on the field near town center.

"I am totally a bit freaked out right now, Meg. And you are the only person who will understand. I know you have seen my mother in action, and now, it is me who you have seen. Or rather felt. Can you please give me more details. I know you told my mom about what happened, but I need to go deeper. To know more. So I can perhaps figure this all out."

"Okay. Right. Let me start back at the beginning. Back when I first met your mom. So, when I first saw it in your mom she was helping Hudson. She thought she was hiding it, but I saw it, right away. There was this glow, this purplish light, that seemed to appear, kind of sandwiched between my cat's chest and your mom's hand. Then she picked him up and made it look like she was pushing the button out by pressing him over her shoulder and patting his back. But I knew, I think, that she did an awful lot more than that."

Meg paused a minute, and Victor was relieved that she had. His head was spinning with so many thoughts he couldn't process anything for a moment. He gathered himself for a bit, as his own memories started spilling out.

"Yeah, I remember when I would fall as a kid, my mom would just put her hands on whatever hurt, and the pain would stop. Pretty sure that I saw that light every time, but I just figured it was normal and that everyone did that. I saw her with the animals, too. She would touch them, look up at the sky and sometimes say words of some sort. Then they would all be okay. Most of the time. They didn't all make it, though. Some things were out of her hands. In those instances, she would be really, really sad."

"Maybe sometimes it isn't meant to be, Vic. Maybe there is only so much she can do. I do remember clearly what happened with my sister, though. Vic, it was a miracle. It was magic. Or more than magic. My sister is completely fine now. Your mom did indeed utter some strange words at the time, too. Just like with Hudson. And I saw that same violet light, both times."

Vic started pacing a bit, impatient for her response. Thankfully she took his cue. He sat down next to her as she began.

"Oh sorry. I skipped over your main question. Anyway, you asked about the details of that day in the woods. Okay. It is really hard to explain. Almost like when one comes out of a dream. Even though I could not see what you were doing, I felt it. I mean I felt the warmth of that light, that purplish light. I felt a bit like sunshine coming through the window at an angle. Refracted light. And Vic, I felt a connection. Like a charge running through me. And then I woke up!"

"I think I get it. And now, looking back, I remember it. It was weird. If felt like that on my end as well. Then all at once, while I was healing you, I flashed back to memories of that feeling when I was a little kid and my mom would make an injury just disappear."

Trying to make what was getting too heavy a little lighter, Meg added. "I guess it must have been 'kiss my boo-boo, Mommy,' on steroids!"

"Real funny, Meg." But he did laugh. Just a little.

Meg continued with a smile. "The whole thing was really weird. But beautiful, too. Mainly because when I opened my eyes I saw that it was you. That you were there and that somehow, maybe magically, you had made me better." Meg pulled him into a hug.

He pulling back a bit, so he could look at her as he spoke the next words. "I am so glad you were okay. I felt so guilty. It was my fault, since I made you come through the woods. I am glad I helped you, although I am sure my mom would have done so as well." He gave her a hug and a kiss, and then looked down at the little blanket of snow that had begun to form near their feet. "But why me? Meg, I don't really get it all. I wish I knew why this all happens."

"Maybe you are supposed to help people, Vic." She leaned back into him and he put his arms around her.

"Maybe. Mom said it comes from love. Maybe I healed you because I love you, Meg." And then all at once he was alone. Standing there, by himself, in the sprinkling of snow.

"Yeah, Vic. Really stupid. Too much. Too soon," and turned around, heading home. Alone and still muttering to himself.

CHAPTER 31

MARY

Mary hung up the phone and grabbed her jacket and mittens and headed out the door. It had been ages since she had gotten the code message. "M&M's four o'clock." That was it. If either girl called, they were to both go to the appointed meeting place, at the time indicated. M&M's was not the candy. It stood for Meg and Mary. They had called themselves that for years. And so Mary knew that she had to head to the bench underneath the streetlight, on Main Street, near the movie theater. She found Meg there already, a bit snowy, but there.

"Come on. Let's go and get a soda," Mary said as soon as she saw her. Brushing the snow off of Mary's shoulders and head like a parent would do to a toddler, she then pulled her up into a standing position. Entering the diner on the corner, they found empty stools at the counter. Mary ordered two egg creams, and then went to put money in the juke box, for the perfect Stones song. Perfect for this moment in time. Plus, it was their mutual favorite. An added plus was that hearing music always put Meg at ease. Mary knew she needed all the calming assistance that she could muster.

Meg spun her straw absentmindedly around the glass. Mary waited, as she knew Meg was about to spout. It took a few minutes but, just as Mary had anticipated, Meg did not disappoint.

"Okay so there are a few things that I just cannot convey even to you and you know that I tell you everything but it has been an incredible week and I don't even know where to start but I think, I mean I am sure, I mean I know that Vic loves me at least that is what he said and I know I feel the same but we have only been dating for a few months and isn't this too early and what on earth should I do?"

Mary, in her infinite wisdom, knew not so say a word. Just yet. Besides, she had to let it sink in herself. This was her most favorite person that wasn't a member of her family, the person she knew almost better than she knew her own self. Her own best friend was admitting that she was in love. Mutual love.

Mary sat there, waiting. Waiting for the next installment. Finally Meg did take a breath, and then she sucked down the entire egg cream. But she didn't utter a word. Wow. This was not the norm. So Mary took the lead.

"Meg, you two are the cutest and most adorable couple. Ever. Everyone hates you." She smiled as she said that, then grabbed Meg's hands in hers. "Seriously, everyone wishes they had what you two have. It is as plain as those cute button noses on your faces that you are in love with each other. We have all, collectively, been waiting for this to finally gel in your own two very stubborn heads. Go for it! He is amazing. YOU are amazing. Why is this a problem?"

Meg just smiled.

CHAPTER 32

MEG AND VIC

To say that their next encounter was awkward was a giant understatement. Not exactly sure how to look at each other, ever since those very serious words were spoken the day before, they both walked along silently, blindly heading through the hallways, eyes looking down. Stopping just outside of Meg's math classroom, neither could take it anymore. Finally, to break the silence, they both spoke at the exact same time. "We need to talk later," said Meg while Vic said, "Let's meet after school." At least they could both laugh at that. He gave her a quick kiss, even though they would get in trouble for it if that incredibly mean and strict vice principal passed by. Neither cared. It would be worth the after school detention. Which they would have to suffer through together. And so, definitely worth it!

After the last bell rang for the day's end, Vic hurried from his final class and met Meg at her locker. "Come. I know where we need to go." Vic said as he grabbed her hand and led her out the front doors of the red brick school building.

"Where are we going?"

"Shhh. Just wait."

He led her back to the gazebo. Sitting down on the wrought iron bench inside, he motioned for her to sit while he paced back and forth for a bit. Finally he came to a stop in front of her and started his explanation.

"I need a do-over. I didn't do that properly yesterday. I am so sorry. I scared you. I know that I made you run away from me."

Meg sat there, silent, looking into his eyes with an unbroken stare.

"Meg, I was just overwhelmed. Finding out about it. You know, IT. It just freaked me out. I don't know how to handle it, or what to do with it. But all I know is that when I saw you lying there and I thought you were dead or something, I just went a little crazy. And I never expected that I would or could actually heal you. HEAL you. Meg it was nuts. This whole thing is nuts. But I know that you mean the world to me. That was a big part of it. That was why I healed you. I do love you, and if anything had happened to you I don't know what I would have done."

He looked so completely vulnerable, so totally adorable, that she stood up from her perch and grabbed him in a giant hug and kissed him. "Vic, I love you too."

He didn't hear her words because he had started on his own ramble at the exact same time. "And my mom and I had a really long talk and she told me that she had the same problem when it all happened to her when she was about my age and wait, what did you just say?"

He pulled back from her and looked down into her eyes, urging her to repeat what she had just said.

"I love you, too, Vic.

CHAPTER 33

SKATING

"How and why are you so good at absolutely everything? You even skate like a pro!"

"Meg, you know, we all have our thing. You are the smartest person I know. Sports just come easy to me. But hey, you skate pretty great yourself!"

"It must be that Canadian gene! Actually my mom put skates on our feet as soon as we could walk. I do love it. Gliding over the lake, just like this, is my favorite winter pastime." Then, a bit shyly, she added in a tumbled rapid fire paragraph, "Truth be told, this is not the first time I ever saw you skate. I used to watch you skating. That is I remember seeing you playing hockey on the lake. I know I also sent an errant puck back to you. Once. Before I knew you. I mean before I met you. Officially. There. I admitted it."

"Yeah, we had pick up games as soon as the lake froze. But wait." They had been skating side by side, but he grabbed both of her hands and started skating backwards, spinning her around like they were in a ballroom. "So you maybe had a little crush on me, even way back then, Miss Meg?"

"Ooh boy, did I! Glad you know now. But I was this dweeb-like little middle schooler. You never would have noticed me."

"Aww, Meg, I wasn't looking. For anything. Back then. Caught up in soccer and hockey games, and hanging with my friends." He pulled them both to a stop and kissed her. "But I most certainly notice you now!"

CHAPTER 34

CARL

"Dad, any progress?" Meg peeked her head into the door to her dad's study.

Carl looked up over his horn rimmed glasses. He hesitated a bit, internally concerned that what might be good news at the onset, could in the end not be ideal. For everyone. "Yes, Meg. A little. My contact is trying to get more information to us. He mailed me another packet this week. It is tricky, Meg, as these are not good times. This Cold War, I am afraid, will go on for some time to come. Anyway, I think Werner Becker might no longer be in prison, based on this information."

"Oh that is wonderful, Dad." She headed over to his desk.

Carl looked up at his daughter, his gray-blue eyes filled with emotion. "I don't want you to get too excited, though, Meg. It looks like he was released, two years ago, but that he had become very ill while incarcerated. I was able to procure some medical records. Although the details are obscure, it appears that he may have been tortured, based on the injuries indicated in his file. Perhaps from interrogation. Infection had set in, and he was, it appears, at death's door. He was in hospital for quite some time.They must have released him from prison, sent him to hospital, and then just let him go home. They most likely figured he wouldn't cause any more trouble after that. Perhaps they expected him to die."

"Oh that is terrible. Wait that means....you mean...is he dead now?"

"No, my Meg. He is indeed alive. But his location is secret. And secure. There is no way, at this time, to ascertain his whereabouts. But I am working on it."

"Dad, what do we do now?"

"We wait, Meg. Perhaps for a long, long time. But maybe it will all come together sooner." When Meg left his office, Carl once again looked through the documents. Concerned that even if they managed to get Werner out of his current situation, it might not be forever. Aksel, his friend, had explained that even if they got him to the states, Werner would undoubtably have to return to Germany. West Germany, though this time. He would, if all worked out, only be granted a temporary visa to the States. This Cold War had its issues. Odds were that he would be forced to leave again once his visa expired. Undoubtedly with his wife and son. His son. This fine young man with whom his daughter was obviously in love. It would break her heart.

CHAPTER 35

MEG

Meg so wanted to tell Vic, to tell him that her father had found his father. But she couldn't. Carl had explained that it would only get their hopes up. It would be excruciating to know that he might just be at arm's length, only to learn that it would be impossible to actually see him again.

So she kept the secret, hoping with all her heart that everything would turn out perfectly. In her mind she envisioned the reunion, where everyone fell into each others arms. Vic could meet his father as his more grown-up self. Elke could be back with her husband. Her one and only love. Vic had told her Elke had never loved anyone else. Ever.

Meg also wanted to tell her mom about Elke. Maybe then and only then would she turn around her cold heart toward the woman, hearing about her life. They both had something in common. The two women had both endured a rocky and difficult past.

December was always a busy month. It was Nutcracker time at the dance studio and Meg had rehearsals almost every day. In between, she had rehearsals for the High School band's holiday concert. She didn't get the chance to see Vic as much, so maybe that made it easier to keep quiet. Even though she wanted to blurt it out every time she saw him, she controlled her urges.

Both Vic and Elke came to see Meg in her Nutcracker performance. She made sure that she had procured the tickets for them on a night when her parents were sure to not be present. Meg's mom still hated the fact that her daughter was dating the son of the woman she detested. But thankfully Evelyn held her tongue, controlling her urges, at least when Vic was around. Carl kept her in check, making sure that she would not do or say anything rash to Vic, but it was not an easy situation. Once Vic was out of earshot, Evelyn would rise to her normal levels of cruelty and would list her usual insults. Meg would just walk away, sequestering herself in her room, and burying herself in a book.

Elke and her son raved about her Nutcracker performance afterward, but in usual Meg style, she downplayed the entire thing, pointing out the fact that she had only been a Snowflake and a Flower in Waltz of the Flowers. She was always just a bit too tall for some of the other roles. But still they lavished praises on her her and told her that she had been lovely!

Meg led them over to Mary. Mary, although just a freshman in High School, had landed the role of Sugar Plum Fairy, and she had been absolutely magical. So incredibly talented, she humbly accepted all the lauded praise. She was destined for a professional career as a ballerina, and they all knew it.

CHAPTER 36

THE HOLIDAYS

The first day of Hanukkah fell on Wednesday the 19th that year, and Meg had so hoped she would be able to give Vic the best present ever, the knowledge that his father had been found. However the days marched on, still with no news. Thankfully the holiday was eight days long, so she hoped and prayed that maybe the information they needed might be there by the final day. Then it was Christmas. Vic came to their home on Christmas Eve, as Meg had so wanted him to experience a traditional Danish Christmas dinner. Her dad was the chef for the meal, and he had carefully prepared roast duck, caramelized potatoes and red cabbage. It was as pleasant as it could have been. Even her mother had been relatively well behaved. That was until just after dessert was served. Her mom had prepared fruit cake and plum pudding, a tradition from her Canadian and British family. But with that dessert came after dinner liqueurs. Evelyn had consumed more wine at dinner than usual, even for her. Then the cordial, the ultimate tipping point, did her in. Unable to contain her typical vile anti-Vic commentary until he and Meg had already left, she spat out her venomous diatribe early.

With glass in hand, she turned to him and spewed out her pent up disgust for him in a slurred and angry voice. "How dare you date my daughter. You, you are a German...You Germans were a terrible lot, not so long ago.. And to top it off you are also a Jew. You are not good enough for my daughter. You.... and that witch of a mother......."

"MOM, stop. Now. It is Christmas." Meg stood up abruptly, and pulled Vic's hand, urging him to leave with her. "That is enough, Mom. Merry Christmas." She said the final words with sarcastic angst and was openly crying by the time she and Vic headed out of the dining room. Vic managed to compose himself, hiding his own disgust at the woman's hurtful words and turned to Carl as he passed him, shaking his hand and thanking him for the delicious meal. Carl's face was tortured, apologetic.

The young couple both overheard Carl's loud and firm voice as they opened the red door to head outside.

"Evelyn, I have had it with you. How dare you say those dreadful words to our guest. He is a fine young man, one for whom you should have much more respect....."

But the words were drowned out as the door slammed shut.

CHAPTER 37

MEG

Creeping out of bed early that next morning, Meg found a little pile of gifts still under the tree, with her name carefully printed on each label. Taking the stack to the couch, she began to open up her presents. She had not come home until after midnight that night before, and the rest of the family had already gone to bed. So, she had missed the event. Happily.

As in the Danish tradition, on Christmas Eve, the family would open their presents. The past year or so they had started limiting giving to only one present per person. Since the girls were now more grown up and didn't need as much, Evelyn had proclaimed this new Christmas edict. It had also made things less stressful. Especially for Evelyn. She hated buying things for other people. It was to be a quick gift opening experience.

Gifts were, for the most part, always practical, and useful, and generally unremarkable. This year was status quo. Still, Meg loved the new soft and silky scarf from Sarah, and wrapped it around her neck. Her mother had given her a run-of-the-mill cardigan, as usual. She kept it folded in its white cardboard box. As she reached for the final gift, the one from her father, he walked in, as if on cue. Clad in plaid bathrobe and slippers, he sat down on the couch next to her.

"Dad, you all didn't wait for me last night." She turned her face up to his, feeling his sadness. "But I was actually relieved. So thank you. I could not have faced her."

"Meg, I figured as much that you would feel that way. Yes, we went ahead, as your mother insisted. She wasn't very manageable and Sarah and I just wanted to get it all over with. Not such a nice way to celebrate. Anyway, she will be asleep for a while. She does need to 'sleep off' last night's overabundance." He kissed the top of her head. "Is all well with Vic? I am so very sorry about things."

"Dad, he gets it. He knows. We had a good talk. Well, actually he managed to talk me down, for sure. I was spitting mad. Dad, she is so mean. Even meaner when she is drunk."

"Yes. Alcohol is a poison to her. As well as an addiction. Although to her, it is a salve. Used to assuage her inner angst. She doesn't connect that what she thinks is helping is actually hurting. One day, I hope we can address her problem, but she has to want to seek help first. As you know, her pride gets in the way. She won't admit it. Until she does, we wait."

"I am so sorry, Dad."

"I am sorry for you as well. Anyway, you have a present to open! By the way, I really like your Vic. He is a wonderful young man, Meg. Anyway, open up!"

She pulled off the paper to reveal a heavy volume. It was a first addition, the history of the Holocaust and its aftermath. Turning to the title page she saw that there was a little handwritten message to her and that it was signed by the author. Even more importantly, the book had been dedicated to Carl Pedersen.

"Wow, Dad, this is impressive! Wait, this is the man who has been helping us? This is the best gift I have ever received! And it was dedicated to you!"

"Meg, as you know, Aksel was my friend, during the Danish occupation. This book was recently published in English, as it was available only in Danish at first. When he told me he would send me my copy, I asked if I could also buy one to give to you for Christmas. It is currently only available over in Europe, for the time being, so he made sure that this arrived in time to give you."

"This is the perfect gift!" Meg hugged the volume to her chest.

"I had so hoped that it would be. It is a monumental book. Aksel was a Danish Jew and he was one of the people whom my friends and I were able to help escape. He in turn helped other Jews, working with us in the resistance. He documented all of the atrocities, during and after the war ended. But he also wrote about the good in people. He described how the Danish people have a decency, a tremendous concern, for the well-being of others. Meg, please always know, that there is good out there. All people are innately capable of good. Even the bad people." He paused for a moment, deep in reflection. "Now, let's go have some coffee and flapjacks. I made the batter last night." He gave her a hug and the two headed into the kitchen.

"Dad, thank you. So much. I will read this cover to cover and will cherish it forever. Merry Christmas, Dad. I love you."

"I love you too, my Meg."

CHAPTER 38

VIC

"Vic, this is way too generous!" Meg had opened the tiny white box, finding two sparkling opal earrings nestled in the soft foam inside.

"Well, they are your birthstone, right? You deserve them." He grabbed her in a hug. "Merry Christmas, Meg!"

"But you don't celebrate Christmas."

"You do, don't you?"

"After Christmas Eve I was kind of trying to forget the holiday." She placed the earrings in her ears, and turned her face towards his. "They are beautiful, Vic. Thank you so much!"

"It is you who are beautiful. Come on, let's go for a walk. I think I should get out of your house. Before your family returns."

It was Boxing Day, the day after Christmas, and the last day of Hanukkah.

"Happy Hanukkah, Vic. And I do have a gift for you. Sort of. I think. But it is not quite ready yet. I had so hoped to have it for you, now, but I am still waiting for its delivery. It might in fact have to be your birthday present. That is only a few days away. Anyway, I have my fingers crossed that the gift will make it in time."

Vic's look was puzzled, but changed to alarm as he heard the front door open. Stiffening, he braced himself, awaiting that piercing female voice. Instead, with relief, he heard an accented baritone. "Meg, are you home?"

"Hi, Dad. Yes, here in the living room."

"Is Vic here?

"Uh huh. By any chance, are you alone?

Carl entered the living room. "Thankfully, yes. Oh hello, Vic! Happy Hanukkah."

Vic stood up and went to shake Carl's hand. "Thank you, sir. Meg and I were actually just going for a walk."

"Oh good idea. I mean, good idea to go for a walk. But I think, instead, that you should actually go straight home. Pretty much now."

"Oh boy, when is she coming back? We had better hurry." Meg stood up, and pulled at Vic's hand.

"She will indeed be home soon. So yes, better hurry so Vic is out of sight. It is probably best that Vic isn't here to experience her, quite so soon. There is only so much one can take in one week." Carl winked at Vic, and led them out to the hall and the front door.

Meg grabbed Vic's coat from the coat rack near the door, and was reaching for her own when Carl touched her arm.

"Meg, I need you to stay home. For a bit. If you don't mind." He gave her a subtle nod over his shoulder as he patted Vic on the shoulder. "Goodbye, Vic. Hope to see you soon. And once again, Happy Hanukkah!"

"We can catch up later, Vic!" Meg gave him a quick kiss and he was on his way.

CHAPTER 39

MEG

As she closed the door, she braced her hands on its red satin surface while she contained herself. Once she was absolutely certain that Vic was out of earshot she let out a whoop and grabbed her father in a fierce hug, trying not to cry.

"Dad! Is it happening? Now? Is he coming? How did you manage this? This is just amazing! Dad, you are the greatest!"

"Meg. He is indeed already here. I think that there is going to be one very happy reunion." Looking down at his watch, he smiled at her. "And that would be right about now! I just dropped him at the Beckers' home after collecting him from the airport. He is tired, and weak, but he is very grateful." Carl took her hand and led her into the living room. "Sit down, honey. There is something that you need to know. But know that it will be for the best, in the end."

She listened, not really wanting to hear. Conflicted, she braced herself for the soon-to-arrive onslaught of opposing emotions. Happy and thrilled by her father's amazing news, she was painfully torn by what would most likely transpire because of that very same happy news. However, in her sadness for her own imminent loss, came the knowledge that there would be a joy in the finding. For the Beckers. This family, after so many years, would now be whole and finally complete. But with that completion, there would need to be a change in locale for them, as the Beckers would not be able to remain in the States. And Meg's love, her very first love, would be taken away from her. Soon.

Composing herself as to not look ungrateful, for her father had indeed moved mountains, she hugged him, more desperately than intended. After one last thank you, she left him before the inevitable eruption occurred. Closing the door to her room tightly behind her, she lay down on her bed and muffled her cries into her pillow.

Thoughts spilled as if from somewhere outside of her brain, thoughts of things that seemingly had no connection to what was happening at that moment. Then the thoughts turned into visuals, wide-awake dreams, spun from somewhere deep in her mind.

From high above, the layer of squishy clouds billows out beneath the plane's wings. Plopped down like dumplings in a stew, the clouds intermittently reveal snapshots of the earth below. Fields and parks and lakes spread below, a patchwork quilt of browns and blues and greens and grays. Pressed against the side of the window, her head begins to vibrate, as the plane begins its descent. And she wonders why and how this giant metal bird can actually manage to fly.

Droning engines work their way into her brain drowning out all other sound around so that she is incapable of hearing even the crying baby three rows back. As she stares down from her perch in the stratosphere she wonders where God is. Is he here somewhere amongst this fluffy white world? Why aren't there any angels, cherubs and seraphim flying around with their opalescent wings catching the light? And the souls. Shouldn't they be here as well?

Why was she remembering this flight now? This flight home from her first trip to Denmark, her first really long flight, years earlier. They had gone over there by ship, to meet her grandparents. However, they travelled home via air as it would have taken way too long to do the voyage both ways. Why was she seeing this in her mind now? Why were these thoughts invading her, now, at this time when everything was changing. When everything had just changed. Completely.

She knew life wasn't a fairytale. And that fairies weren't real. Or were they?And then another vision comes into her mind. From the summertime, the very first summer that they had spent at their cottage in Port Severn. That was when Fairies were real to her. Once. At least for a moment or two.

Sitting on the wooden deck, engrossed in a novel, she is suddenly startled by a lovely greenish and luminescent being. Gracefully fluttering about her head, it dangles its legs down like pointed dancers feet. She has to share this, has to let someone else know! Running into the cottage, she calls to awaken her sister Sarah, who is immersed in a late Sunday morning sleep.

"Sarah, come quick. There's a fairy outside. A real fairy! I promise!"

"Yeah, right, Meg." Sarah pulls the covers back over her head.

"Your loss." She returns outside to be with her fairy again. Only this time she finds her fairy perched against the side of the cottage, opened wings revealing its true nature, its true identity. A Luna moth, she discovers. It is only a moth. Crushed, she heads back inside.

Meg so wanted life to be surreal. She yearned for Luna moths to be fairies, and to see angels floating in the clouds. But life was real and sometimes harsh. Sometimes a fairy tale was simply just a fleeting fantasy.

EPILOGUE

Startled and not really sure exactly what it was or where the incessant ringing noise was coming from, she put down the bucket of oats and headed into the cottage. Once she had realized that it was actually the front door causing all the racket, she trod angrily across her freshly mopped floor to answer it. Furious now, she realized that she had just tracked snow and grit throughout the entire house.

No one ever rang the doorbell. Never locking the door, ever, she had never really heard the bell before. The ringing had risen to a persistent crescendo as whomever was out there was pushing it over and over and over.

In a burst of frustration not normally present in her, she whipped open the door, speaking in a tone foreign to her demeanor. "Can I help you?"

"I certainly hope so!" She knew that voice. She would always know that voice.

"Oh my God! Werner!" Clutching the edge of the door to brace herself from collapsing as her trembling legs offered no viable support, she found herself staring at the man whom she assumed she would see never again.

Werner. Older, grayer, and thinner. But it was Werner. The shaking in her knees had worked its way up through her entire body. It felt like even her hair was shaking. And then, the tremors disappeared, as if they were never there, just as soon as he spoke her name.

"Elke."

They fell into an embrace as a tall and lanky blond teenager walked through the kitchen door.

Coming Soon!

Hwin and Little Bear

by
Inger Margaret Foster

The Artist

Chapter one

A blank canvas. Intimidating yet oddly comforting at the same time. Open for interpretation, the surface presents itself as an entity soon yet to be. It waits patiently for that first brush stroke. With that important initial contact of bristle to fabric, direction is given. Setting the course for all of the others, that maiden stroke guides and leads and encourages the strokes that follow.

Jessica had two canvases with her, one on the easel and the other propped against her paintbox. Carefully stretching them the night before, she had applied a generous coat of gesso. Twice. The second time she added cadmium yellow light to the creamy white consistency. Underlying yellow was her trademark, her secret ingredient that helped generate and create the luminosity that the next layers of paint would eventually emit. Each and every work began with an inner glow. The rest of the painting just followed suit.

The sun had just risen behind the rolling hills and she sat back a bit in her folding chair to survey her surroundings. Last night she had dreamed of the painting she was about to create. It always happened that way. An idea would start, just an inkling of an idea, early in the day, and then, that night while deep asleep, the idea would expand and grow and wrap itself around her. Like a clinging vine it would envelop her mind, gently pulling her ideas together. The following day it would all be there, ready to go. Without a struggle, her hands would generate what her mind had designed.

She had chosen the location days earlier, but had been there in the afternoon. Noting where sunrise would occur, she knew that she needed to arrive much earlier for the perfect light. She had gotten up before daybreak and hiked to the exact spot. Sipping tea from her steaming thermos, she watched a layer of fog just rising from the little crimson and gold sunlit lake. And the pasture in the foreground sparkled with dew. A liver chestnut horse was peacefully grazing, just to the left of the lake. No imaginary thinking could have created the vista better than the one that was presented to her by nature itself. Instead of sticking to her initial plan, she let what was unfolding before her just be. Now, only minimally changing direction, she would begin to interpret what was lying in front, translating it into her own distinct style. As stunning as the vista was, she would maintain the inner emotion, capturing exactly how she felt in that moment in time: Serene.

Zipping her lightweight jacket, guarding against the still chilly air, she set to work. Sketching the composition in charcoal, she kept her mind focused on the direction of light and the shadows that occurred. She had a photographic memory and the vision would be indelibly marked in her brain. No need to photograph it like many of her fellow art students did. She would complete the underpainting there and would finish the piece over the next few weeks, tweaking it until it attained her own precise standards.

Blocking in the colors, she worked quickly, placing everything in order. Her palette was already set out with warm colors on one side, cool on the other. Balancing the two helped achieve her trademark luminosity even further. She had perfected her method combining the techniques of the Impressionists and Vermeer, the Master of Light. But in the end her style was all her own. Somehow, she had humbly shrugged off the overall consensus that she was indeed a prodigy.

At the age of fifteen, when people sang her praises, calling her gifted, she was frankly embarrassed by the whole thing. And she felt guilty claiming credit for what came so easily to her. For her work came from somewhere within. It was as though there were a light that dwelled deep inside of her, and she was simply listening to it, interpreting it onto her canvases. Finishing the first steps as the sun rose a bit higher and the light began to change, she started packing up her paints. Standing, she folded up her chair, and organized the items so that it wouldn't be too cumbersome heading home. Now that she had a wet canvas, she had to be more careful. Her one last peak at the view lasted a bit longer than she anticipated as she noticed movement in the pasture. The horse who had been so very still earlier, the perfect addition to her middle ground, was now moving. Slowly, the mare headed towards the wooden fence, working her way towards what could only be described as a vision.

Quickly, but quietly, Jessica started down the hill, towards what she had seen from a distance, trying to make sense of it. Maybe it was just that morning light playing tricks on her eyes, but, incredulously, it appeared to be an angel. A tiny cherub. Clad in a soft and flowing white gown, the daylight shining behind her, the figure was reaching her tiny hands up to pet the nose of the horse. The horse, looming so high above the angel, lowered her head, ever so gently, allowing the contact to occur.

Closer now, Jessica hid behind a tree so that she wouldn't disrupt the scene in front of her. For it was indeed a scene, one that could have been shot for a movie. It was that perfect, that transcending. As the sun rose a bit higher, the two creatures were shrouded by the aura of diffused sunlight, emitting an unearthly glow around them. Creative mind spinning, Jessica wanted to race back to her other canvas and paint this exquisite moment. Transfixed, though, she was incapable of moving a muscle.

All at once the spell was broken. A voice calling into the mist broke the magic. "Mandy, Mandy, where are you?"

The little angel turned and ran, tiny bare feet skipping over the dew laden grass.

With special thanks to

Heidi Rose Sealfon

for being the real life inspiration for Elke.

INGER MARGARET FOSTER

ABOUT THE AUTHOR

Born in Montreal, Quebec, Inger and her family immigrated to the United States in the early 1960's. Growing up in the quiet suburban town of Ramsey, New Jersey, she attended Ramsey High School, where she developed her love for both writing and art. Later on, as an art major at William Paterson University, she eventually earned her Masters in VisualArts, with concentrations in English and Education.

Immediately after college, Inger worked in sales, first for Clinique and then for Eastman Kodak. After marrying her husband Nick, she relocated to Westchester County, NY. In 1986, she began teaching at Saint Patrick's School, in Yorktown, NY where she still substitute teaches today.

Inger returned to her love of writing after her children headed to college. Essays became short stories, and the short stories eventually evolved into her first novel, The Final Canoe Ride. The concept for The Final Canoe Ride was to be a triptych, from the onset. Starting out in the middle of the trilogy, the reader first meets Meg, a woman in her late forties who is struggling with an unexpected onset of breast cancer. Through dreams and flashbacks, Meg's back story is developed, a story that is to be explored again throughout the trilogy.

Split Soul, the sequel, gives subtle glimpses into to Meg's life, mystically and unconventionally through the eyes of others. Taking place in London, Split Soul begins with a woman named Beth Barrows who is dealing with a frightening and unusual case of amnesia. On her journey, she retraces the steps of another in order learn who Beth actually is, this woman in whose body she is currently dwelling. Both stories are searches for self and soul, with the main characters linked as they travel on parallel paths.

Elke's Magic, the prequel to The Final Canoe Ride, gives insight into young Meg's life. Touching on the poignant yet often humorous awkward years, Elke's Magic is filled with the rewards of friendship and the pangs of first love. Taking place in the early1970's. Elke's Magic also walks the reader through the underlying prejudices and persecution still lingering, years later, brought on by World War II.

Inger is married and living in Northern Westchester County. She is the mother of three amazing adult children and two wonderful daughters-in-law! Inger and her husband Nick love to travel, especially throughout Europe and to Florida and to their little cottage on the Georgian Bay, in Ontario, Canada.

Please follow Inger Margaret Foster on Goodreads, Facebook, Pinterest and on her Amazon Author Page, or you can find her on http://hwinandlittlebearpress.com.

Hwin&LittleBearPress